Praise for

SCARLET
AND
IVY

"This is one of the best books I have ever read. It was exciting, funny, warm and mysterious." **Lily, aged 9**

"The whole book was brilliant... after the first paragraph it was as though Ivy was my best friend." **Ciara, aged 10**

"This book is full of excitement and adventure — a masterpiece!" **Jennifer, aged 9**

"This is a page-turning mystery adventure with puzzles that keep you guessing." **Felicity, aged 11**

"A brilliant and exciting book." **Evie, aged 8**

"The story shone with excitement, secrets and bonds of friendship... If I had to mark this book out of 10, I would give it 11!" **Sidney, aged 11**

SOPHIE CLEVERLY was born in Bath in 1989. She wrote her first story at the age of four, though it used no punctuation and was essentially one long sentence. Thankfully, things have improved somewhat since then, and she has earned a BA in Creative Writing and MA in Writing for Young People from Bath Spa University.

Now working as a full-time writer, Sophie lives with her husband in Wiltshire, where she has a house full of books and a garden full of crows.

Also available:

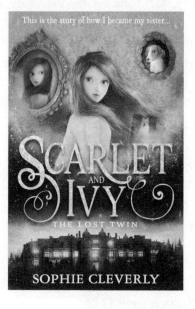

SCARLET AND IVY

THE WHISPERS IN THE WALLS

SOPHIE CLEVERLY

HarperCollins *Children's Books*

First published in Great Britain by HarperCollins *Children's Books* 2015
HarperCollins *Children's Books* is a division of HarperCollins*Publishers* Ltd,
HarperCollins *Publishers*
1 London Bridge Street
London SE1 9GF

The HarperCollins *Children's Books* website address is
www.harpercollins.co.uk

2

978-0-00-758920-3

Printed and bound in the United States of America by
RR Donnelley

Find out more about HarperCollins and the environment at
www.harpercollins.co.uk/green

In memory of Sir Terry Pratchett.

"Do you not know that a man is not dead while his name is still spoken?"

ALIS GRAVE NIL

NOTHING IS HEAVY FOR THOSE WHO HAVE WINGS

ROOKWOOD SCHOOL MOTTO

Prologue

y name is Scarlet Grey, and until today I thought I would be lost forever.

I was taken away from Rookwood School in the dead of night, locked away in an asylum and given a new name. They told me I was crazy. They told me I'd imagined everything that had happened.

Everyone else forgot about me.

Everyone but my twin sister Ivy...

I couldn't believe my eyes. I thought I was seeing my reflection on the other side of the window. And then she moved.

She put her hand up against the glass. For a minute, I just stared. Our eyes met through the window, and I held up my own hand – a perfect mirror image.

I was *saved*!

Throwing the doors open, I ran outside, Nurse Joan calling after me. I skidded to a halt and hurled my arms around my twin.

"Ivy! Is it really you?"

She looked back at me, and immediately burst into tears.

Maybe I should have cried too, but I couldn't. I'd never been so happy. I could've flown off the ground at that moment. She'd found me, I was being rescued, I was getting out of the asylum. I was *free*.

So instead, I laughed. I laughed and I span my sister round until she had no choice but to laugh through her tears, and we both collapsed by the pond in a heap.

"Oh, Scarlet," she sobbed. "Miss Fox told me you were dead. I... I believed her, I really did. Father believed you were dead too. But then I found your diary, and I pieced it all together, but still I... I never thought..."

I realised then that we weren't alone. The nurse and the secretary had stepped outside, but that wasn't all.

"Miss Finch!" I jumped up. "Why are *you* here?"

My old ballet teacher was staring at me, happiness and

shock mixing in her wide eyes. "Hello, Scarlet," she said. She ran a hand through her red hair and exhaled loudly. "I can't believe this. You *are* alive. I think I need to sit down."

I guided her to a bench, and she sank down awkwardly. "When I get hold of my mother..." she muttered.

Her mother?

Ivy clambered up from the ground, still shaking and clearly torn between smiling and sobbing. "We'll get you out of here," she said.

Reality came crashing down around me. What if the doctors wouldn't let me go? What if they still thought I was insane?

I turned to my twin. "Did it all really happen?" I asked quietly. "All of it? Violet's scheming? The fight on the rooftop? Miss Fox taking her away?"

Ivy stared back at me for a moment, and then she nodded. "All of that, and more..."

Miss Finch went back inside with the secretary. I almost tried to stop her going, half worried that they'd persuade her to leave me here. But she said she would set things right and get me discharged.

Ivy and I sat shoulder to shoulder on the bench next to the pond. It was just like we'd done so many times at our aunt Phoebe's house when we'd stayed there as children, long

11

before Ivy went to live with her.

Once I'd convinced her that I was all in one piece, Ivy told me everything that had happened. I learnt about how she'd been forced to go to Rookwood and pretend to be me, the hunt for the diary entries, her new friend Ariadne, evil, money-hungry Miss Fox and her secret daughter: Miss Finch.

For the first time in my life, I was speechless.

When she'd finished, I was gaping like one of the goldfish. Finally, I managed to say something.

"You know what this means?"

"What?" she said.

"I'm a GENIUS. My plan actually worked! You found the trail I left you!"

Ivy gave me a withering look. "*You're* the genius?"

I grinned.

"What's happened to you?" she asked, her face suddenly slipping back into concern. "This place, I can't imagine..."

I wasn't ready for that question. I frowned, feeling sick. Despite everything, I was free, that was all that mattered now, wasn't it?

"Please," she insisted. "I need to know."

A thought occurred to me. In the pocket of my horrible regulation grey smock, I had something that could answer all her questions. Wordlessly, I handed it over.

I am insane.

At least, that's what they tell me. I didn't believe it at first. Of course I wasn't insane. I knew what I'd seen. Her name was Violet, and Miss Fox made her disappear. I was there. I'd written it all down, hadn't I?

Doubt crept in. They said I was having delusions, that I'd dreamt up a scenario on a rooftop, where a teacher had made a girl disappear. Doctor Abraham told me it couldn't be true. Why would a teacher do that? It didn't make any sense. It was a delusion, created out of my dislike for Miss Fox, he said. All I had to do was admit that I'd made the whole thing up and they'd consider sending me home.

Well, I wouldn't admit it, obviously. And I'm not even sure that I want to go home. Of course I want to leave this living hell, but my father and stepmother haven't so much as written me a letter. If they know I'm locked up in here, then they don't care a jot. The only person who cares is Ivy, and she can't possibly know. Because she'd come to get me out if she did.

Wouldn't she?

So, anyway, the days pass. They keep calling me Charlotte, no matter how many times I tell them that's not my name. I have a tiny room, like a cell, with bars on the windows. It's painted this horrible shade of mint green that makes me want to vomit. But I've spent so much time staring at the walls now that I could draw you a picture of every crack and every paint bubble and every tiny strand of spiderweb.

I have to see Doctor Abraham at noon on weekdays. He says I have a "mental disease", but honestly he seems to think being a girl is enough of a mental disease on its own. For the first few appointments I just screamed at him and knocked his papers off his desk, demanding he let me out, and all he would say was, "You're being hysterical, Charlotte".

Hysterical! I'd like to see how he'd react if he were locked up in here and people tried to act like it was for his own good. "SCARLET!" I yelled back at him. "My name is Scarlet!" It didn't seem to help.

I no longer have a diary. My old one, the lovely leather-bound book with SG scored on the cover, is now in pieces around Rookwood, where I prayed my twin Ivy would find it. Once upon a time Ivy had one the same, only with her initials, but she was always too busy with her nose in other people's books to write down her own story.

I begged and begged the nurses for a notebook to write in, and finally Sister Agnes gave in and brought me this one that she'd only used a few pages of. It was just grocery lists and dull things like "must send that package to Aunt Marie in Dover", so I tore out the pages and made them into tiny paper planes, which passed a good half hour in this place, where the days are long and empty.

I wish I knew how long I'd been here. Until today I had no way to count the days. I tried scratching marks into the paint, but it had been done by so many inmates before me that I couldn't keep track of my marks.

But... I'm not like them. Some of them are truly disturbed, they cry and shriek all the time, and I don't.

It's just... sometimes, I think perhaps, just maybe, the doctor is right. Why would I be in an asylum if I was perfectly sane? Maybe I just made up the whole thing.

I dreamt that I had a twin who would always be there. I dreamt that I was my father's little girl, that he wouldn't let anyone hurt me. I dreamt that there was a girl named Violet who disappeared into thin air.

The only way that I'll know if it was all real is if Ivy finds me. But it's been so long now... it could be too late. The trail I left could have been destroyed; Miss Fox could have found it and tossed it into a fire.

I must have hope. Ivy will find me. She'll come.

I know it.

I watched the tears roll down Ivy's face.

"You did it," I said. "You found me!"

She tossed the tatty notebook aside and swept me into a bone-crushing hug.

"I'm never losing you again," she promised.

Chapter One

SCARLET

It's not easy having to tell your father that, despite him believing the opposite, you're not dead. But looking on the bright side: at least I was alive to tell him that.

Ivy and I knocked on the door of our childhood home the day after that first telephone call from the asylum (a lot of silence followed by a lot of shouting). Miss Finch had managed to get the school to pay for a room in a boarding house while everything was sorted out and Father made his way back from London.

It was a cold day at the beginning of November, and we

stood shivering on the steps of the cottage.

The door was opened by a hideous she-troll.

"Oh. There's two of you again," she sneered.

"How nice to see you, dear stepmother," I replied, pushing past her.

She huffed indignantly at me as Ivy followed me in. "Scarlet, if you think you can walk around like you own the place just because of what happened, then you've got another thi—"

She froze mid-sentence at the sound of heavy footsteps on the stairs. Suddenly she put on a different expression like a mask, and pulled us into her arms. "Oh, girls," she simpered. "I'm just so glad to have you home safe."

Father stepped down into the hall. When his eyes met mine, he took a deep breath and adjusted his tie.

"Scarlet," he said.

"Father."

"I just... I can't believe it. You're here." His normally cold exterior was showing some cracks – tears glinted in his eyes. I broke free of my stepmother, ran over and embraced him. He wrapped his arms around the back of my head, not quite touching me, but it was closer than we'd been in years.

Ivy hung back. "We need to tell you everything," she said. "Rookwood isn't just awful, it's dangerous. And what Miss Fox did—"

Our stepmother snorted. "It's all over now, isn't it? This *Miss Fox* has run away. There's no need to trouble your father with such things."

Father straightened up and looked at his wife. "No, Ivy's right," he said. "I want to understand how this happened. Let's go to the study."

He led us away from her, and I couldn't help feeling a little amused by how horrified she looked at being left out of the conversation. Why did she want to avoid the subject of what had happened, anyway?

We walked through the house, past familiar doors and fireplaces and furniture. The landscape of my childhood. Harry, one of my young stepbrothers, peered round a door and stuck his tongue out at me. What a way to welcome your sister back from the dead! I reached over to give him a slap, but Ivy grabbed my wrist and pulled me past.

Father's study was still dull and sparsely furnished, with a mahogany writing desk, a chair and some filing cabinets. Ivy and I sat down on the floor, beside the fire that half-heartedly smouldered in the hearth.

Father sat in the chair and began polishing his glasses.

"I don't know where to start," Ivy said.

"I do," I replied.

I told him everything that had happened. I told him about Vile Violet, my roommate who had bossed me around and spied on me and stolen my things. I told him about wicked Miss Fox, who had taken Violet away after she threatened to reveal a dark secret up on the rooftops. I told him how I'd tried to confront Miss Fox, only for her to smuggle me out of school and have me locked up in the asylum.

Father stared intently at the wall above my head, but I could tell he was listening from the sharp intake of breath every time I got to a shocking moment.

Ivy chimed in towards the end, telling him what had happened at Rookwood in the meantime. I'd heard more of her story in the boarding house and on the train. How Miss Fox had hidden me away to save her own skin, to stop anyone finding out that she had an illegitimate daughter. Not to mention that she was funding her lifestyle with the money paid by parents as school fees (perhaps explaining why the only thing on the dining hall menu was stew).

"It was a nightmare, Father," I finished, "and I'm just so glad to be home. So can we stay?"

He looked at me. "No."

"Why?" I gaped at him.

He took off his glasses and put them down on the desk. "Scarlet, you know why. You've got to go back to school."

I felt a wave of unease wash over me.

"But Father, someone from that school put Scarlet in an *asylum* and pretended she was dead," said my twin. "You can't send us *back* there!"

I looked at her, surprised that shy, timid Ivy had spoken out for once. But our father didn't seem to notice. "It was just that Miss Fox character. And she won't be returning."

I stood up, fists clenched. "I won't go back there! You can't make me!"

Father didn't rise to it. "Edith hasn't got time to run around after you two. She has the boys to think of."

Edith. Our stepmother. I hated the way he said her name. It was clear he cared about her more than he cared about us.

I heard Ivy mutter something at the carpet.

"What was that?" Father asked.

She climbed to her feet. "I said, are you sure *Edith* wasn't involved with this? She was the one that told us Scarlet was... you know... She was the one who identified the body, wasn't she? She offered to take care of the funeral arrangements, everything..."

Our father went deathly silent, and for a second I thought he was going to slap her. But his breath came out shakily and then he spoke again. "Don't be foolish. She cares for you. We both do. That's why we want to see you get an education, and become independent young ladies."

Ivy stared at the floor, and I knew she was remembering the first time he had said that. The first time he sent me away.

"Father," I said quietly. "Don't. Don't send us back to

Rookwood. Please."

He shook his head. "I know you've had a difficult time. I'll think about it."

Father ushered us out of his study, leaving us standing in the hallway. I gritted my teeth, and contemplated giving his door a good bashing. But then I spotted Harry's gormless face staring at me from the parlour door.

I ran over and into the room. He tried to duck down behind the armchair, but I grabbed him by his collar and pulled him up.

"What are you up to, you little weasel?" I demanded.

"Nothing!" he said, scrabbling and trying to get away.

"I bet you were eavesdropping, weren't you?"

He kicked me in the shins. I was momentarily distracted and dropped him. "I wish you'd go away again!" he yelled, running to the other side of the room and trying to flatten out his scruffy hair. Which was pointless, because it always looked like a bird's nest.

"You little..." I started, raising my fist. Ivy clutched my arm.

"Mummy *hates* you," he said. "We've all been better off without you. We've actually had money and I got new shoes and—"

He probably would've continued that sentence, but I barrelled towards him. I tried to grab him again, but he

22

ducked under my arms and ran away shrieking. *Ugh. What a hideous brat.*

In the suddenly quiet parlour, Ivy spoke.

"Scarlet," she whispered. "I think I might have been right. I think our stepmother *was* involved with this. If they had more money, maybe that's because she was bribed by Miss Fox to go along with it."

I squeezed my fists so tightly that I could feel my nails digging in. "I *bet* she was. That disgusting TROLL. I'll kill her! I'll—"

Ivy interrupted. "But say it *is* true. How did Miss Fox know that our stepmother wanted us out of the picture?"

I felt my cheeks turn hot. *Of course.* There was something I'd forgotten. "Ah. My first day of school. We *may* have had a small argument in front of everyone, including Miss Fox. I *might* have been a bit insulting to our dear stepmother, and she may have started yelling that I was a leech and it would be better if I disappeared forever."

Ivy sat down heavily in the armchair and put her head in her hands. "Scarlet," she said finally, her voice muffled, "are you saying at least some of this whole mess was just because you can't control your temper?"

I shrugged. How was I to know that Miss Fox would turn out to be so evil that she'd try and convince everyone I was dead?

*

After what seemed like an age of Ivy trying to calm me down, I decided that we should go to the garden. Down past the thorn bushes and out into the thin woods, there was a winding footpath that led to a clearing and a babbling brook. It was a special place for us. A good place to escape to.

As we walked past the study door, I heard raised voices. It was Father and Edith. I came to a stop, Ivy nearly walking into the back of me.

"...HAVE to send them back." The sound of our stepmother's voice floated through the door. I leant up against it, and reluctantly Ivy did the same. "They need to grow up."

"I'm just not sure, dear." That was Father. "Do we really think they'll be safe there?"

"They'll be fine," snapped our stepmother. "It's just a school! I can't COPE with them here, you know that. They need to go." And then, the killing blow. "It's them or me!" she screeched.

"Her," I whispered. "Say her!"

There was an unbearable pause.

When Father replied, his voice was quieter, and I strained to hear it. "I'll take them back in the morning," he said.

We were allowed to stay for supper and had a bed for the night, but that was all. Father was shipping us back to

Rookwood first thing the next day, a fact that had left me spitting with anger while Ivy tried to comfort me. Father left me to "get used to it". He was lucky I didn't snap his stupid glasses in two.

Our stepmother dished up burnt roast lamb and soggy vegetables for dinner, whilst simpering about what brave girls we'd been. Harry and the other boys, Joseph and John, didn't seem to care that we'd ever gone away, and were their usual horrible selves, pulling faces and flicking peas at us. I scolded one of them and the troll flicked her eyes up at me, nostrils flaring, as if I'd attacked him. But she didn't dare say a word in front of Father.

Exhausted, Ivy and I made our excuses and climbed the steep stairs to our bedroom. I flicked on the little brass light switch, illuminating the two matching beds side by side, and the tall mirror between them. There was a cupboard and some curtains, but besides that the room was bare.

I carried my suitcase inside, a small leather one that contained a few of my possessions. Much as Miss Fox had been a repulsive witch, she had at least allowed me that much when she threw me into Rosemoor Asylum. She must have told the doctors so many lies about me to convince them I was hysterical, a fantasist, and needed to be locked away for my own sake and for the safety of others. I shook my head fiercely. I was *never* going back there.

"Oh, Scarlet," said Ivy, sinking down on to her bed. A little cloud of dust flew up from the white sheets. "What are we going to do?"

I flopped onto my own bed. "Poison Edith? Run away?"

"No poisoning, Scarlet. And we can't run away from everything. We don't have any money, or a motor car. They'll just catch us and send us straight back to Rookwood."

"We'll dig an escape tunnel," I said. But I was being stupid, and I knew it. We were stuck.

My twin gazed up at the plaster on the ceiling. "It could be worse."

I *hated* Rookwood. Every inch of the place was filled with terrible memories. "How could it possibly be worse?"

"I could be alone."

She smiled at me then, a smile that flowed from the depths of sadness, and I felt a piece of my anger float away.

"You're right," I said. "We're together. That's all that matters."

I jumped up on the bed, shoes on, not caring.

"If we have no choice but to go back, then we're going back. Rookwood School isn't going to know what hit it!"

Chapter Two

Ivy

For months I had believed my sister was gone forever. And now she sat beside me, as we rode in a motor car back to a place neither of us wanted to set foot in, and I had to remind myself that she was real. I kept reaching out and taking hold of her arm for reassurance.

Father's car was comfortable but smelled strongly of pipe tobacco – he insisted on smoking all the way there. He attempted conversation, awkwardly. "How did you get on with your lessons, Ivy? How's your ballet coming along?" As if that was all there was to talk about.

I felt myself getting more and more nervous the nearer we got to Rookwood. I'd only been gone a few days, but knowing what had really happened made the place even more intimidating and foreboding than it had been before. I had to tell myself it was all right – I had Scarlet, I had Ariadne, and Miss Finch was on our side. Miss Fox was gone and she wasn't coming back.

The car chugged through the school gates, the stone rooks on the pillars poised to grasp us with their talons. Scarlet squeezed my hand tightly, but when I looked up at her, her expression was as determined as ever. The tall trees bent over us, their crisp leaves peeling away in the late-autumn wind.

When we came to a stop in front of the building, Scarlet pulled away from me and got out of the car without a word. I leant out and watched as she climbed the steps with her suitcase. I didn't know if she would ever forgive Father for this.

I stayed in the car. If this was my one chance to speak to Father, I had to take it. "Do we have to do this? Do you have to just drive away and leave us here?"

He craned his neck to look at me as I perched on the rear leather seat. "We've been through this, Ivy."

"I know, but there has to be another way. What if we went to stay with Aunt Phoebe? She must be lonely."

Father got out and pulled open my door with a *thunk*. Then he crouched down at my feet, looking up at me, a gesture that made me feel like I was a little girl again. "I know you're worried about things being as bad as they were before." He looked up at Scarlet, who was staring pointedly at the stonework above the entrance. "But it's all in the past now. We have to move forward. The headmaster, Mr…"

"Bartholomew."

"Bartholomew, that's it. He reassured me and your stepmother that everything will be in order; that it's all been dealt with. You need an education and this is the best place for it. Your sister can pout all she wants, but one day she'll realise that we did the right thing."

I looked down at him, kneeling there on the gravel, greying streaks in his dark hair and wrinkles in his suit. The little girl in me wanted to give him a hug, tell him how much I'd missed him. But I wasn't that girl any more.

So instead I just said: "You're wrong."

I picked up my suitcase and pushed past him. I heard his gasp of shock, but I wasn't going to back down. Not this time.

"I love you, girls," he called out from behind me.

I didn't look back. I climbed the stone steps and took Scarlet's hand. She pulled me through the entrance, and we left Father far behind.

*

"HOW DARE HE?" Scarlet yelled, as the door shut behind us. "How dare he act like this is all for the *best*?"

Rookwood's worried secretary looked up and shushed her, though it was one of the most timid shushes I'd ever heard.

My twin didn't pay even the slightest bit of attention. "That old hypocrite! He lets the boys run around doing whatever they like, but we get left here to rot. After everything!" She kicked the wall. "This is so *unfair*!"

"Ahem..."

I looked round. It was Mrs Knight, the head of Richmond house, standing on the other side of the hall. "Kindly leave the wall alone, Miss Grey. And perhaps save all of our ears by keeping your voice down?"

"Sorry, Miss," I said. Scarlet just frowned.

"We've been expecting you, girls – Mr Bartholomew has been making arrangements. I'm to take you to his office now." She gave me a smile, but it was an uncertain one. "Miss Carver will arrange for someone to take your suitcases to your room." She indicated the secretary, who was regarding Scarlet warily.

I shot my twin a look to see if she'd caught that – were we sharing a room? She raised her eyebrows at me.

"This way," said Mrs Knight, as we deposited our suitcases by the front desk. It was Sunday morning, so the classrooms she led us past were empty, silent as if they were sleeping. In a low voice, she added, "I hope you can put your ordeal behind you, Scarlet, and have a fresh start. We were all so horrified to learn what Miss Fox had done." Scarlet made a face, but she didn't reply.

My heart pounded as we neared Miss Fox's office, and I saw to my surprise that its door was wide open. There were men inside in suits, looking through her files. The hideous stuffed dogs remained, glassy-eyed and grotesque.

Thank goodness Miss Fox was gone. I hoped Father was right, and that Mr Bartholomew would make everything better for us.

Before I had time to think more about it, we'd come to another heavy wooden door with 'HEADMASTER' in stern capitals on the nameplate.

Mrs Knight knocked gingerly. Her knock was answered with coughing, and a rasping "come in". She waved us inside, and I hoped she'd follow, but instead she just quickly pulled the door closed behind us.

This office was big. Twice the size of Miss Fox's. A huge stone fireplace in one corner sheltered a roaring fire, and dark furniture loomed in front of wood-panelled walls. There were no windows.

An oak desk took up almost all of the floor space, and behind it was a tall leather-backed chair with a man sitting in it, silver-haired and hunched over. A quivering hand pulled a pocket watch on a chain out of his jacket. "You're late," he said, and his voice rattled like bones.

Scarlet and I looked at each other in horror.

He gestured for us to sit down on two chairs in front of the desk, and we did so immediately.

He spoke slowly without really looking at us, like he was considering each word. I watched his eyes, sunken and hollow. "Girls, welcome back to Rookwood. I understand there have been... troubling times. But I can assure you that these are now over."

Then he was silent. I wondered if I should say something. "Thank you, sir?" I whispered.

Almost to himself, he continued, "I always questioned whether I was right to leave a woman in charge of my school. Now I know the answer to that."

I gripped Scarlet's hand under the desk, just in case she was going to start shouting at him. But she remained tight-lipped.

"You must understand, the school is the thing. Teachers and pupils come and go, but the school remains. That is what matters."

We both nodded. Where was he going with this?

"Rookwood needs its reputation intact in order to survive. We are nothing but the image we project to the world."

Evidently Scarlet had had enough of biting her tongue. "Is there a point to all this, sir?"

Mr Bartholomew unfurled in his chair. I realised as he drew himself up that he was a very large man indeed. His eyes narrowed at my twin. "I don't remember asking you a question, Miss Grey."

I shrank back, but Scarlet was undeterred. "You didn't, sir."

"THEN WHY ARE YOU TALKING?" he roared.

Scarlet blinked. I felt like my heart had stopped in my chest.

And then the headmaster folded back again, coughing.

When he finally spoke, his voice had returned to its previous volume. "Rookwood prides itself on our education system, our high standards of teaching and the safety of our pupils. You will not do anything to compromise this. But –" another cough – "I assure you that what happened will not be repeated. Not on my watch."

We sat there, not wanting to say a word.

"That is all. You may go."

"What was that all about?" I asked Scarlet, when I'd overcome the shock.

"Search me."

We walked towards the stairs, and I had that strange

feeling once again, doubting that my twin was really beside me. I'd never walked these halls with her before. "Do you think we can trust him?" I asked, as we climbed the staircase.

Scarlet laughed sarcastically. "Trust him? He looks like a *vampire*!"

I risked a smile. "At least he's not Miss Fox. And he obviously doesn't like her. Perhaps he'll come clean to the school, tell everyone what's really been going on."

"He might. I mean, people are surely going to notice that there's two of me all of a sudden."

We'd just reached the top of the stairs when someone came barrelling into me and knocked me backwards on to the carpet.

"IvyohmygoshIvyyou'reback!"

I looked up, stunned, and saw a familiar grinning face.

"Ariadne!" I cried.

"Hello!" my friend scrambled up, pushing her halo of mousy hair out of her eyes. "I'm just so pleased to see you! And –" she turned and took in the sight of my twin, who looked frankly baffled – "Scarlet! Scarlet's here! You found her, you really did it!"

Ariadne started bouncing up and down to the point where I felt mildly seasick. But nevertheless, I was truly, truly pleased to see her again. I grinned and clambered up from the scratchy floor. "Yes, I did it. Well, *we* did it."

"*Who is this?*" said Scarlet in a mock-whisper.

"Oh, um..." I held out my hands to both of them. "Scarlet, this is Ariadne. She helped me find you."

My sister frowned, but Ariadne didn't seem to notice. "Nice to meet you!" she said brightly. "Ariadne," she repeated, "like in *Theseus and the Minotaur*."

"Who and the what?" said my twin rudely

"*Scarlet*," I said meaningfully, "we need to get to our room and..." I looked at Ariadne, and a horrible realisation dawned. There were only two beds in our dorm.

I looked back and forth between my twin and my best friend. Ariadne's smile had faded to something that was only a fraction of her usual cheeriness. "Oh yes, about that. Mrs Knight said I had to move." She looked at the floor. "I'm to have a new roommate, apparently."

I felt crushed. Scarlet appeared not to notice – she was too busy glowering at passing students that were staring at us. "I'm so sorry, Ariadne. I didn't even think about this."

"It's no bother," she said, though I was pretty sure it was. "We'll still see each other every day. Can I come and sit in your room now, while you unpack?"

I nodded. "Of course."

And then I grabbed Scarlet before she could get us into further trouble, and we headed back to room thirteen.

Chapter Three

SCARLET

eturning to my old room was like a dream. One of those where you go to somewhere you know well, only for it to be strangely different and unsettling.

It was the same old room thirteen, but none of my things were where I'd left them. The left side of the room was completely empty, presumably where this Ariadne girl had cleared her things out, while the right side was littered with Ivy's possessions. "I always chose the right side," I said aloud. "Well done, sis."

Ivy smiled half-heartedly. I think she was annoyed at me

for not being very polite to her new friend. But it was her fault, really. I'd heard her side of the story and I knew all about Ariadne, but I didn't have to be happy about it. Ivy had been supposed to keep everything a secret. How had she known that she could trust this girl?

I picked up some of the books from the right-hand bed and plonked them down on the left.

"What are you doing?" Ivy asked from the doorway, Ariadne leaning around her with a puzzled expression.

"Sorting things out so I have the right, you have the left."

Ivy raised her eyebrows at me. "We're still doing that?"

"Of course. And besides, *this* bed has the hole I keep my diary in." I went over to my suitcase that had been deposited just inside the door and pulled out the flimsy notebook I'd been given in the asylum. "You should really try keeping a diary, Ivy. You never know when it might save your life."

"True," my sister conceded. She traipsed over to the other bed, Ariadne following behind her like a lost puppy.

I got down on my hands and knees and stuffed my new diary into the familiar hole in the mattress. I wasn't sure if it would be safe there any more – of course I could trust Ivy, but I didn't know Ariadne one bit. But then I wasn't exactly in danger now. Was I?

"Who's your new roommate, Ariadne?" asked my sister.

"I don't know," the mousy girl replied. "I asked Mrs

Knight, but she just made a funny face and walked away. Who do you think it could be?"

"Probably just some new girl," I said, since everyone else would have a dorm already. "I'm sure they'll be *great*. You won't want to hang around with us at *all*."

Or at least I hoped not, because Ivy and I will always be a team of two, no more.

Ivy started pulling things out of her suitcase and laying them out on the bed. "It'll be dinner soon. Maybe you'll find out then."

I grimaced. There were many horrors at the school, and the dinners were one of them. But at least it wasn't hospital food, which had tasted like despair.

There was a knock at the open door. We all looked round.

It was Nadia Sayani. I glared at her, thinking she'd come to pick on me, but to my surprise Ivy and Ariadne greeted her warmly. Clearly a lot had changed while I was away.

She did a double take upon seeing me and Ivy side by side. "So there really are two of you," she said, slightly breathless. A smile spread across her face. "Well, I never... Twins! Or did your reflection just walk out of the mirror, Ivy?"

Ivy smiled at her. "Yes, that's definitely what happened."

"Ha! Well, I came to tell you that Mr Bartholomew has called an assembly," she said. "Before dinner. We all have to get down there now."

That was unusual. We never had assemblies on Sunday, nor at this time of day. "Who told you?" I asked.

"Mrs Knight," Nadia replied. "She asked me to run round and tell everyone."

Ariadne jumped up. "Maybe he's giving out prizes!"

I wasn't so sure. "Or canings..."

We filed into the assembly hall and sat down on the uncomfortable wooden benches. Looking around, I spotted Miss Finch on a chair at the side, and she smiled at me. The stage was empty, though – no sign yet of Mr Bartholomew.

I leant over to Ivy. "Do you think he's going to tell everyone what happened last year?" She shrugged, and pointed at Miss Bowler, the swimming teacher, who was glaring at me from the other side of the hall. We weren't supposed to be talking, apparently. "But he's not even here y—"

My sentence was interrupted by a loud cough echoing around the walls, and suddenly the headmaster appeared on the stage. The teachers shushed everyone into complete silence.

"Good afternoon, girls." He spoke in the same slow, dragging manner that he had done in his office. "Some of you may not know me, as I have been away for some time, recuperating from an illness. I am Mr Bartholomew, the headmaster of Rookwood School. My father was the founder of this school, which he set up to provide a proper education for his daughters, as well as those of his important, influential friends." He paused, coughed into a dark red handkerchief, and then carried on. "You may be wondering why I've called an assembly at this hour."

There was a murmur of agreement.

"I have been informed that there were some incidents while I was away."

I nudged Ivy. "He's going to tell everyone about Miss Fox!" I whispered. Miss Bowler waggled her finger at me, but I ignored her.

"Well, I can assure you, now that I have returned, we are going to be doing things *my* way. Severely delinquent behaviour will be punished with immediate expulsion. I will have nothing going on –" he paused, cleared his throat – "nothing in this school that is not directly sanctioned by me. Is that clear?"

Everyone murmured their agreement, but it clearly wasn't enough for him. "I said, IS THAT CLEAR, girls?" His gravelly voice could reach a surprising volume, and several girls around me flinched.

"Yes, sir!" we chorused.

"The prefect system will be reinstated, since it has been neglected in my absence. I will be selecting representatives from Richmond, Evergreen and Mayhew houses to be my prefects. They will be making sure that everyone follows my rules."

Ivy was looking at me, and I could tell we were thinking the same thing. Wasn't he going to say anything about Miss Fox and what she'd done? Surely that was more important than picking prefects?

Mr Bartholomew started pacing up and down slowly, and said, "We will keep the past in the past, and look towards the future. And to that end, I want to welcome two students."

I looked around. *New students*?

"Ivy Grey, stand up, please."

My sister looked horrified. But she stood up, trembling a little as the eyes of the whole school fell on her.

"Miss Grey will be joining her twin sister, Scarlet. Everyone welcome Ivy, please."

There was a mumbling of welcomes, but everyone was still looking at Ivy strangely. Not least me, who was wondering what on earth our headmaster was playing at. Why was he pretending that Ivy was new? Why was he covering up what Miss Fox had done?

"And we have another student who has returned from spending some time abroad," Mr Bartholomew continued in his rattling drone.

He pointed to the back of the room. I turned round, following his finger. "Miss Adams, please stand up as well."

I couldn't believe it.
Vile Violet.
She was back.

Chapter Four

IVY

I had never seen Scarlet look as horrified as she did at that moment. Her complexion went a strange shade of green when Mr Bartholomew called out Violet's name. I sat down again and grabbed hold of her hand.

But then Violet looked awful too; pale and frightened. I'd never seen her before, but I felt as if I knew her from Scarlet's diary entries. She'd seemed like a horrible bully, someone to be afraid of, but at that moment I only felt pity for her.

I hadn't known that they'd found her. I hadn't even

been certain that she was still alive. Perhaps Miss Finch had tracked her down too, or Mr Bartholomew himself. If she'd been locked away in the asylum like my sister... Well, wherever she'd been, she certainly hadn't been "spending some time abroad". The thought made me queasy, and I had to look away.

The headmaster had finished the assembly with boring notices and some reminders of Rookwood's many rules. *Lights out at nine o'clock sharp. No food in bedrooms. No running in the corridors. In fact, no running anywhere, except perhaps on the running track.*

I still couldn't believe that he was persisting with Miss Fox's deception, claiming that Violet had been away and I was a new student. What exactly was he playing at? I supposed that the school's reputation was being put ahead of us, ahead of *me*, yet again.

And it meant more lies. Just when I thought I could be myself again, I'd have to act like I hadn't already been here for months.

We traipsed to the dining hall, where the familiar chatter and clatter enveloped us. I could feel people staring in amazement. I supposed we were a startling sight – perfect mirror images of one another.

"Oh, Rookwood food, how I didn't miss you," I said to

my stew as we sat down, before realising that, according to the headmaster, I'd never eaten it before. I glanced round, hoping no one had noticed my comment. I thought Scarlet might nudge me and tell me to shut up. But she was distracted, staring at the other side of the Richmond table.

Violet was standing there, and she looked *miserable*.

Mrs Knight was talking to her. "Miss Adams, I'm afraid you'll have to join the Evergreen table."

Penny jumped up. "But Miss, she was in Richmond before! Can't we just kick someone else out?" Penny had been Violet's best friend, not to mention another of Scarlet's worst enemies.

Our house head frowned. "There's simply no room now that Ivy and Ariadne have joined us. And besides, there are several free places in Evergreen."

What? Suddenly Mrs Knight was talking about me as if I were a new student, too. She knew full well what had really happened. Why was she going along with the headmaster's game?

Scarlet spoke up. "She should do as she's told and go and sit with Evergreen." And then in a dramatic whisper to me, "As far away from us as possible."

"Miss Grey, will you mind your manners?" snapped Mrs Knight, exasperated.

I looked at Violet, expecting her to start shouting at any

moment. But to everyone's surprise, she simply walked off to the other table without a word.

Penny sat down again, looking stunned. I could tell she was wondering what had happened to her old friend Violet. The one that ordered everyone else around and wouldn't be told what to do by anyone.

I picked up a forkful of the unappetising stew and stared at it. Oh well, I *was* hungry. I ate some, and it was at least hot. Someone had gone overboard with the pepper, though.

Ariadne appeared beside me with her dinner. "Did I miss something?"

"Violet was sent to the Evergreen table," I said.

Mrs Knight's gaze flashed to Ariadne. "Miss Flitworth, your room has been arranged. You will be staying with Violet."

Ariadne's eyes went wide. I almost choked on my stew.

"I trust there won't be any problems?"

Ariadne shook her head slowly, but she didn't blink. "No, Miss."

Mrs Knight nodded, and then turned to talk to Madame Lovelace, the history teacher.

Oh gosh. Poor Ariadne, subjected to Violet. It had been bad enough reading about what the girl had done to Scarlet, making her life a living hell – I really hoped that history wasn't about to repeat itself. But so far, Violet seemed to be giving everyone the silent treatment.

Penny glared at Ariadne and me and started to say something, but then Scarlet kicked her under the table. "Ow!" she muttered, reaching down to rub her leg.

"Scarlet," I said in a quiet warning tone. "I want to actually finish my dinner tonight."

My twin grimaced at me. I mimicked her own grimace back at her. At least some things never changed.

After dinner, I left a despondent Ariadne at the door of her new room. I wished her good luck, and she gave me a hug. There was no sign of Violet.

I had one of the school's traditional lukewarm baths and then climbed into bed – almost climbing into the wrong one, as I instinctively walked towards Scarlet's.

"Mine," she reminded me from the dressing table, where she was brushing out her hair.

I folded myself into the sheets, exhausted. I half-wondered if any of Ariadne's collection of sweets remained under the bed.

Scarlet turned a new page in her notebook and started writing, her hand moving quickly across the page. I smiled sleepily. I could've only imagined this sight a few months ago. When she put the book away, she saw me watching. "Nosy," she laughed.

I laughed back. "Need I remind you that reading your diary was the most important thing I ever did?"

My twin grinned at me. "Doesn't mean you can make a habit of it." She came and stood at my bedside, yawning in her nightgown. "Budge up."

"Eh? I thought you said you wanted your old bed back?"

"I know what I said. But just this once I—" She looked at the floor.

"Want to know you're not alone," I finished. We'd always slept in the same bed when we were little.

Scarlet nodded, looking unusually sheepish.

"Oh, all right. But please don't snore." I moved over, leaving just enough room for her.

We went to sleep, back to back, a perfect mirror image once again.

The morning bell rang out and I sat up in bed with a jolt.

Scarlet was already up and pulling on her school dress. She prodded me gently on the shoulder. "Lazy bones!"

I pushed her away playfully and wriggled out of the bed sheets. The air was chilly on my skin. I rubbed my eyes. "Wait. Do I have a uniform now?"

She nodded and flung open the wardrobe to reveal a uniform that matched hers. At least someone had thought of that – perhaps it was Miss Finch? Thank goodness someone was still looking out for us.

I got changed as Scarlet darted around the room putting things in her satchel, humming a tune. I dreaded having to pretend that I was a new pupil again. I'd spent so long pretending that I *wasn't* new. How could my twin be so carefree, after all that had happened? Sometimes I felt as though I understood her, and other times she was like a complete stranger.

As I sat down at the dressing table to lace up my shoes I caught sight of myself in the chipped mirror. *Scarlet,* I thought immediately. But my twin moved behind me, breaking the spell. *No, Ivy,* I had to remind myself. I was me again. I wasn't sure if there was a me to go back to, though. I'd spent so long pretending to be Scarlet that maybe the old Ivy had faded away.

Later, Scarlet enthusiastically ate her breakfast, gulping down the lumpy porridge that I felt quite sure she hated. I was puzzled at her cheerful manner, but gave up worrying about it when Ariadne sat down next to me.

"How was Violet?" I asked.

My friend shrugged, and she looked as puzzled as I did. "I honestly don't know. It was like she wasn't even there. I kept trying to talk to her, I really did, but she didn't say anything. I just went to sleep in the end."

"Strange. I missed having you in room thirteen."
I noticed Scarlet frowning at that. I realised I shouldn't have
been talking about Ariadne and I previously sharing a room
as I wasn't even supposed to have been at the school, but
everyone else was too busy chatting amongst themselves to
notice.

Ariadne sighed. "If only we could all stay together. If I had
a genie, I'd wish for it."

"Don't waste your wishes," I warned her. "You *could* wish
for us not to have to go to this school."

"Or for a million pounds," said Scarlet, pointing a
spoonful of porridge at me. "No one could tell us what to do
if we had a million pounds."

"I bet Mr Bartholomew could," I said. We all thought
about it for a moment, and then shuddered. There was just
something about him, in his words and his voice and the
jerky way he moved. I felt sure that he was someone we didn't
want to cross.

Chapter Five

SCARLET

I was terrified.

Terrified of returning to lessons. Terrified of Violet. Terrified of Miss Fox being out there, *somewhere*.

Terrified of Rookwood School.

I barely slept a wink that first night. Whenever I dozed off, I had terrible nightmares. When I was awake, I kept thinking I could hear things *in the walls.*

But was I going to tell Ivy that? *Not likely.* I had to be brave for her, because I hated the idea of her being as frightened as I was. So I'd jumped out of bed and acted like it was the happiest day of my life. I even wolfed down the disgusting porridge, though I had no appetite and my stomach was in knots.

Morning assembly was at least not too scary, as all we had to do was sing hymns and listen to Matron's lecture on keeping our dorm rooms tidy. But there was something surprising – a letter arrived addressed to me and Ivy.

"It's from Aunt Phoebe!" Ivy exclaimed when she saw the postmark. As Ariadne hurried off to the first lesson, we stood in the hallway reading it.

Dear Scarlet and Ivy,

I was so overjoyed to hear the good news. It's truly a miracle to have Scarlet back with us. I wish I could see the two of you together again. But I fear it is not to be. I hoped that you would be able to stay with me, but I see now that I have interfered with your lives too much already. Edith is right, you need to complete your education and not be held back by some old biddy like me. I'm very sorry. I hope I will see you again someday.

With all my love and best wishes for the future,
Your aunt
Phoebe Gregory

There were tear stains on the paper, and they'd smudged some of the ink.

I dug my nails into my hands. "Did our stepmother make her do this?"

Ivy's excited expression had faded, and now she looked like she was about to cry. "I suppose so."

I took the letter out of her hand and screwed it up. "It's nonsense! *She's* the one who's interfering, not Aunt Phoebe. That *witch*!"

Girls were staring as they streamed past, but I didn't care. They could stare all they liked.

I would get our stepmother back for this one day. I still suspected that she had persuaded our father that I was dead after being bribed by Miss Fox. But she wouldn't be able to control our lives forever.

We walked into the history classroom side by side. I *hated* history. I didn't see why we had to learn about things that dead people had done.

There had been some rearranging of the desks, and I saw to my horror that Violet had been given the one next to mine.

"Ah yes," said Madame Lovelace, covered in dust as always. "We have a twin joining us. Which one of you is Ivy?"

"I am," I said quickly.

Ivy looked at me like I'd just declared I was a radish.

"Oh good. Welcome to Rookwood School. I hope you have a better aptitude for history than your sister," she declared, glaring at Ivy, who squeaked in frustration. But she went along with the swap and took the seat next to my arch-enemy. "There's a spare desk over there. Here, take a textbook."

"Thank you, Madame," I said politely. I took it from her and headed to the back of the room, as far away from Violet Adams as was physically possible.

As we sat down and Madame Lovelace started writing names and dates on the blackboard, Ivy turned to face me. "What are you doing?" she mouthed.

I pointed repeatedly at the back of Violet's head. Finally Ivy seemed to get the message and turned back round.

I watched as my twin studiously copied from the blackboard. I wondered if this was how she'd behaved when she'd been pretending to be me. I never did anything studiously.

At least this time it didn't really matter if we acted like each other or not – Madame Lovelace was blind as a bat, and not particularly observant even with her spectacles on. So instead of doing my work, I started drawing in my jotter instead. I drew myself, dancing, and then I drew Ivy next to me. Ballet was the only lesson I was looking forward to. At least Miss Finch knew the full truth about what had happened – there was no chance she would pretend that Ivy was new and I'd never been away, like Mrs Knight was.

I was still doodling when the bell rang for the end of class, and almost jumped out of my skin. Penny noticed and laughed. I pulled a face at her and gathered up my things.

Ivy frowned at me as I headed to the front of class. "You can't just do that, Scarlet," she said, when we'd left the classroom.

"Do what?"

"Pretend to be me!" she snapped.

"I didn't want to sit next to Violet."

"Well, can you give me some warning next time?" And with that, my twin shot ahead of me through the crowds.

Fine, I thought. *If she wants to be alone, she can be alone.* I turned round, intent on storming off in the other direction.

And came face to face with Violet.

I was rooted to the spot. I couldn't breathe as it all came flashing back to me. *The freezing rooftop. The fight. Miss Fox dangling her over the edge.*

Was she going to hit me? Scream in my face? Promise revenge?

But no, her eyes were blank as if I were invisible to her. "Excuse me," she whispered absently.

And she walked straight past me.

*

I tried my best to pull myself together for the rest of the lessons that day, but it was difficult when my twin was clearly still annoyed with me. I didn't understand why she was so cross. She'd already had plenty of practice at playing my role, so why was it a problem now? I thought she didn't want to have to pretend to be new.

We retreated to room thirteen to get changed into our leotards. "I don't know what's got into Violet," I said. "She's not her usual awful self at all. She's not really *anything*. Just *blank*."

Ivy sighed. "I don't know what's going on."

I thought she'd say something about how Violet had probably been through an ordeal that had affected her, how we should be grateful that she wasn't trying to murder me. But she just sighed a little more loudly and continued pulling on her tights.

We ran down to ballet (well, *I* ran, and Ivy just walked quickly, keen not to break any rules). Miss Finch greeted us as we descended into the chilly basement.

"Welcome back, Scarlet," she said to me quietly and with a smile. "I trust you haven't forgotten your warm-up?"

I shook my head. "No, Miss."

"Good. And be on your best behaviour, please." She looked pointedly at the piano. I hoped my embarrassment didn't show.

Miss Finch smiled at Ivy, too, but didn't welcome her to the class. Ivy looked grateful for that.

I took hold of the *barre* next to my sister and began my exercises, right leg first, then left leg.

It was something so very simple, but it felt like coming home. When I practised ballet, I wasn't just Scarlet any more, I was Scarlet, the world-famous prima ballerina of the future. My destiny stretched out in front of me. And with Ivy by my side, no matter how cross she was, everything felt complete.

My bliss was interrupted by Penny whispering in my ear. "You may be back, but I haven't forgotten that we've got unfinished business, Scarlet Grey. I'm going to find out why Violet won't talk to me, and if it's got anything to do with you then there'll be trouble."

I frowned at her. "Why would it be my fault?"

She elbowed me viciously. "*Supposedly* she went to some school in France, lording it about while *you* were locked away in an asylum. Yet she's gone all weird and silent while you're just fine and dandy! And the teachers are acting like Ivy is a brand new pupil and you've been here all along! Something doesn't add up."

I wasn't fine, but Penny didn't know that. "I'm *brilliant*, thank you. Now leave me alone." I moved into *rond de jambe à terre*, moving my leg in a half circle, intent on ignoring her.

"Listen, scum," she spat. "I want my friend back. And I will do whatever it takes, do you understand?"

I said nothing, but I felt my insides turn to ice. I knew just how far Penny would go.

Chapter Six

IVY

That night I woke up, and Scarlet was gone.

I'd been fast asleep until a boom of thunder rattled the window and jolted my eyes open. A lightning flash lit up the room a moment later, and I saw that her bed was empty.

The storm didn't frighten me, but Scarlet's absence did. For a moment I thought that she was still dead and I was alone at Rookwood School again.

But no, I was in the opposite bed, there was no Ariadne and I could see my twin's leotard and ballet shoes dangling off the chair. I breathed a sigh of relief.

So where was she?

It felt like some time that I was lying there, staring at the door. Finally the handle turned, and Scarlet crept back in.

She jumped when she saw that I was looking at her.

"Where did you go?" I whispered.

"Nowhere," she said. And then, "I just went to the lavatory."

"Ah," I said, relieved.

She climbed back into her own bed, and I drifted back to sleep, listening to the storm raging outside.

When Scarlet and I got down to breakfast the next morning, Ariadne came rushing over to me with her tray. "I just overheard Mrs Knight talking to one of the other teachers. She said there's been a theft! Apparently Mr Bartholomew is furious."

My ears pricked up at this. "Oh? I wonder what was stolen?" *At least it wasn't us this time*, I thought, our escapade in the kitchens springing to mind.

And then I remembered.

Scarlet had left our room last night, and I couldn't truly say how long for.

I watched my twin as she sat down with her porridge. She

must have heard Ariadne, but she didn't say anything. Had she been involved?

"Honestly, Mrs Knight sounded really scared about how angry he was." Ariadne frowned. "Her hands were all shaky. I think she's afraid of the headmaster. Do you think that's why she's going along with him, telling everyone that you're a new pupil? He can't be as bad as Miss Fox, can he?"

I shrugged. I didn't want to think about it. But if Mrs Knight was scared of him, well... perhaps that did explain why she wasn't telling everyone the truth about me.

"There's going to be an assembly about it," Ariadne continued. Her lip started quivering. "I hope I don't get a caning."

"Why would you?"

"Well... I was eavesdropping..." She cringed, as if she'd admitted to some sort of hideous crime.

I laughed and patted her on the back. "I know this school has a lot of rules, Ariadne, but I don't think there's one about that."

"Oh, phew."

I turned back to Scarlet. "Scarlet, do you know anything about what's been stolen?"

"No," she said, chewing a mouthful of her breakfast. "Why would I?"

I frowned. I had a feeling my sister was keeping something from me.

It was Mrs Knight who took the stage at assembly. That was a relief, at least. I was in no hurry to see Mr Bartholomew again.

"Girls, I'm afraid I have a serious matter to discuss. There was a theft last night." Cue the collective gasps of everyone except me, Scarlet and Ariadne. "Now, since there was no break-in, we have to presume that one of you is responsible. I have to say, I am deeply disappointed."

Someone near the front raised their hand.

"Yes, Liza?"

"What was stolen, Miss?"

"Clothes belonging to Penelope Winchester. They were taken from the laundry."

Now it was *my* turn to be shocked. I looked around and located Penny, a few rows behind me. She looked *livid*.

Suddenly I was even more worried. Scarlet and Penny's dislike for each other was legendary. Penny had been horrible to her just yesterday. What if my twin was out for revenge?

There was a flurry of whispers, and Mrs Knight waved her arms to quieten everyone down. "We take thefts very seriously at this school, and if the culprit is caught then they will be –" she paused, swallowed – "duly punished."

Scarlet's face was blank, not betraying anything.

Mrs Knight looked down at the piece of paper she was holding. "The headmaster wants you to know that he will be keeping an eye on you all, and increasing the levels of discipline if necessary." For a moment, a horrified look passed over her face, and then she regained her composure. "And to that end, I have a list here of the new prefects. Prefects will be responsible for reporting to the headmaster if they witness anyone breaking a rule." She unfurled a piece of paper and cleared her throat. "Miss Winchester is the first to be appointed."

Several people groaned, and before I could catch myself I was groaning as well. Penny was sure to be a nightmare as a prefect.

Scarlet was no longer expressionless – now her eyebrows were narrowed and her cheeks were puffed out.

The list went on. "Maureen Alcott. Lettie Clark. Dot Campbell. All of these girls have been recommended for their exemplary behaviour. If you have been selected, please report to Mr Bartholomew this afternoon."

When we left the hall, Scarlet sped out past me, not saying a word.

Ariadne grabbed on to my dress. "Isn't this awful? Penny as a prefect? I mean, I thought we'd reached some kind of agreement with her, but she's being as nasty as ever."

"And now someone's stolen her clothes." I frowned. "She'll probably be even worse than usual, trying to find out who did it."

"I don't understand why Mr Bartholomew would pick her. He is... he's so..."

"Strange?"

She nodded, mousy hair bobbing.

I sighed. "I think everyone here is."

At lunchtime I found I couldn't keep quiet any longer. It had been playing on my mind all day – was Scarlet the culprit?

It was a pleasant day after the night's storm had exhausted the rain clouds, so I led my twin outside and under an enormous oak tree at the back of the school.

"What do you want, Ivy? I assume you didn't drag me all the way out here to make daisy chains."

"No, I want to know what you're playing at."

"I'm not playing at anything," she snapped.

"You were out of our room last night. If you didn't steal Penny's clothes, then—"

"What are you talking about? I *didn't* steal Penny's clothes! Why would I? Who do you think I am?"

"Well, you've got to admit it looks suspicious."

"No," she said, "it doesn't. Because I'm your twin, and you shouldn't *suspect* me."

"You haven't really given me a reason not to!" I retaliated. "You have a history of keeping things from me. *Important* things. Or have you forgotten what you got up to last year?"

Scarlet turned away, arms crossed and fuming. She wasn't going to forgive me for this. I should have given up, but I told myself that I wasn't going to let her walk all over me for a moment longer. "Don't ignore me!"

She didn't look round. "I don't have to explain myself to you. I'll do whatever I want."

"You *can't* just do whatever you want!" I tugged on her shoulder until she had no choice but to face me again. "You wanted to get into this school *so badly* that you switched our entrance papers. That's the reason all of this happened in the first place! But now you've got what you wanted and you're just wasting it by getting in trouble all over again!"

"You don't understand!" she shouted back. "And you never will!"

And with that, she stormed off, and I was alone.

Chapter Seven

SCARLET

After half-dozing through lessons and a tepid dinner, it was night-time once more. I wouldn't talk to my twin, and she didn't seem keen to talk to me, either. I waited for her to drift off to sleep, even giving her a poke in the shoulder to double check, and then I pulled out my new diary from its hiding place. Rookwood School was an eerie place at night, drenched in shadows and silence. I didn't even know if I *wanted* to keep a diary any more. But it was better than lying sleepless in bed, especially when I knew what nightmares may come.

Girls with blank faces locked away in the walls, banging with their fists, screaming to be let out...

That was why, the night before, I'd got up and wandered to the lavatories. But even that had scared me. It was safer to stay in bed.

Dear Diary,
I wish I was somewhere else. Anywhere else.

I wrote those words and stared at them. What else was there to say?

Ivy thinks I stole Penny's clothes, but I didn't. I wish I had, because the look on her freckled face was priceless. But I wouldn't do it, not really. I'm not a thief.

Why doesn't Ivy trust me?

I only left the room because I couldn't sleep. This place scares me. But I needed to prove to myself that I could walk its corridors and nothing bad would happen to me.

I sniffed and tried to pretend that there weren't any tears in my eyes. I looked up at the tall dark windows, raindrops pouring down them in sheets. The words just didn't want to come. This wasn't me. Scarlet Grey didn't get *scared*.

Thump.

What was that?

I sat bolt upright.

Thump.

The room was almost pitch black, but I could just make out the lump that was Ivy under her covers and hear her snoring softly. I was safe. Nothing was going to get me in here.

I just had to keep telling myself that.

Wednesday morning dawned, and the morning bell was like a hammer to my head. If Ivy had noticed I'd been awake, she didn't say anything about it. But then she didn't say two words to me anyway.

And it didn't look like things were going to get any better when Mrs Knight once again called an assembly.

"It greatly saddens me to tell you that there were yet more thefts last night. A good deal of food was stolen from the kitchens, and –" she paused and looked down at her sheet of paper as if she couldn't quite believe it – "Miss Jones tells me that books have gone missing from the library as well. Really, girls, this is appalling!"

A ripple of murmurs spread through the hall, and I knew everyone was speculating about who the thief was. *I heard something in the night*, I thought. *Maybe it was the thief.*

I turned to my twin, about to whisper to her, when I saw

her furrowed brow. Ugh. It was no use. She'd probably think I was just trying to cover my tracks.

"Thieves will not be tolerated in this school. If you know anything about who might be responsible, please report it to myself or Mr Bartholomew immediately." Mrs Knight carried on giving notices, and then read a story from the Bible and told us all how it was bad to steal. As if we didn't *know*.

Well, I supposed one person didn't.

Who could it be?

At the end of assembly, I saw Penny march up to Mrs Knight and start whispering something to her. I kept an eye on her as I stood, ready to leave, and saw her point very clearly in my direction.

The little leech! She was telling on me! And for once, I hadn't even done anything wrong. I looked around for my twin to share my disbelief, but she had already walked out.

I stood, momentarily glued to the spot, but Mrs Knight beckoned me over. Despite the rising panic inside me, I smiled calmly and tried to look as innocent as possible.

Penny gave me the stare of death as she walked away from us. I would *not* let her pin this all on me just to earn herself a few house points. *Perfect prefect Penny*. I shuddered.

"Scarlet," said Mrs Knight, "Penelope thinks you may

know something about the recent thefts. She thinks you have some sort of grudge against her."

"Please, Miss. She's the one with the grudge against *me*. I haven't done anything."

Mrs Knight sighed. "Honestly, I think you're both as bad as each other. Run along, then," she said. "But you need to be careful. If there's any evidence against you, Mr Bartholomew is going to come down on you like..."

"...a ton of bricks?" I finished, having received that threat many times.

She fixed me with a stern, searching look. "Perhaps make that two tons," she said.

Even though we didn't have ballet that day, I wanted to talk to Miss Finch. Ivy was still cross with me, and I barely knew Ariadne. If there was anyone who might be on my side, it would definitely be Miss Finch. She'd helped to rescue me, after all.

I lurked on the ballet studio stairs at the end of the day, arms folded, waiting for her lesson to finish. Eventually, once the gaggle of older girls had left, she noticed me standing there.

"Hello, Scarlet," she said, peering up the stairwell at me. "Are you settling back in well? How's Ivy getting on?"

"I didn't do it," I said.

She blinked at me. "That's nice. What is it you didn't do, exactly?"

"I'm not the thief, I mean. Everyone thinks I am, but I'm not. I swear!"

She nodded gently, and then indicated for me to come down into the room. I followed her to her piano stool, and she perched on it. Her bad leg meant she had to rest often. "I believe you."

"Will you vouch for me?" I asked. "Tell the other teachers that I didn't do it?"

She played a few keys on the piano, the way she sometimes did when she was thinking about things. "Scarlet," she said after a moment, "like I said, I believe you. And I don't think you'd lie to me. Not any more." A pointed look. She was thinking about the piano-smashing incident. I felt my cheeks flush. "But I'm also not sure if me telling everyone will do any good. Especially not if there's evidence against you."

"There isn't any!" I snapped back. Then I sighed and leant against the shiny new piano. There was something important I'd remembered. "Besides, Miss Finch... I'm not the only one who hasn't been completely honest. You never told us that you were Miss Fox's daughter!"

She rubbed her face, and I saw in that moment just how tired she was. "We all have our little lies. Sometimes they become big ones. Sometimes you have no choice but to hide the truth, even when you know it's wrong."

I nodded. "I know what you mean." Lies were hard to keep under control.

She smiled at me cautiously, and went back to playing the piano. I took that to mean the conversation was over, but there was something else I needed to say. I cleared my throat and her hands stopped moving. "Miss... Thank you for helping Ivy find me. I'd still be locked away if it wasn't for you. And, well, *I* wouldn't have wanted anyone to know if Miss Fox was my mother, either!"

Miss Finch looked as if she was about to say something, perhaps to confide in me, but with a shake of her head she let it go. The moment hung in the air, empty of words. And then she finally spoke.

"Thank you, Scarlet. I know it seems as if Mr Bartholomew is brushing everything that happened under the carpet. And some of the other teachers are going along with it and pretending Ivy is new. But you can always come and talk to me if you're finding things hard. *Both* of you. Look after each other, Scarlet."

Chapter Eight

Ivy

"I'm not the thief," Scarlet said to me that night as we climbed into our beds. I hadn't spoken to her throughout dinner, as I knew I'd only ask about the thefts again. But now she had brought it up, and I needed to say something.

"All right, look," I said, leaning up on one elbow. "I want you to swear that you didn't steal those things."

Scarlet glared at me, but eventually her pride gave way. "I swear," she growled. "I swear on our mother's grave.

73

Happy now?"

I wasn't particularly happy, but I had to believe her. As suspicious as some of the evidence was – I could easily believe that Scarlet would take Penny's clothes just to annoy her – taking any of Rookwood's terrible food and books was rather pushing it.

"If it's not you, then who is it?" I asked. "Who would want to take all those things?"

"I don't know," said Scarlet. "But I *will* find out."

Hmm. Scarlet certainly was determined. That was probably a good sign. If she was intent on finding the culprit, then perhaps it really wasn't her.

At the same time, I knew my twin wasn't a saint. Not by any stretch of the imagination. She was so offended that I hadn't believed her, but with some of the things she'd got up to in the past, well...

My thoughts were interrupted by a brisk knock at our door, before it swung open without a pause. It was the matron. "Lights out, girls," she said, flicking the switch and leaving us in the dark.

I stared at the ceiling, and tried not to imagine Scarlet sneaking away in the night.

Despite my efforts to stay alert (just in case Scarlet did disappear – but she wouldn't. Of course she wouldn't), I dropped quickly into a dreamless sleep. When I awoke to the sound of the morning bell ringing, it was to my immense disappointment that I was still in Rookwood. It was never a great place to find yourself.

We walked to breakfast, Scarlet yawning the whole way. I gave her sideways glances, and couldn't stop myself from wondering if she was tired from roaming the school at night, getting up to no good.

"It's such an honour to be a prefect," said Penny, as we sat down with our bowls of porridge. She was preening in front of her friends, showing off the little red notebook she'd been given to write down all our misdeeds. "Mr Bartholomew chose me *personally*, you know."

I didn't think I'd want to be chosen for *anything* by Mr Bartholomew. Not that I would say that aloud. But unfortunately, my twin never had as much tact as I did.

"If you want to be a personal slave to the teachers, go ahead!" she said, rolling her eyes.

Mrs Knight was dumbstruck. "Really, Scarlet!"

Scarlet just stuck out her tongue and then carried on eating her breakfast. I fought the urge to sink my face into my porridge.

Mrs Knight stood up and walked round to Scarlet, giving her a clip round the ear. "Ouch!" Scarlet cried, though I could see it hadn't been that hard.

"Mind your manners," the teacher said.

"Yes, Miss," Scarlet grumbled back. But somehow, I doubted that was a promise she'd remember to keep.

That proved true later, in our Latin lesson. The teacher, Miss Simons, a round-faced woman with incredibly long red hair, was reading out conjugations. She tapped a ruler down the list on the blackboard as she came to each one. "*Facio! Facis! Facit!*" There was no sound in the room but the tapping and the seemingly endless list of verbs that we all had to copy down. At least, not until I heard loud snoring coming from the desk beside me.

I looked over at Scarlet. She was fast asleep on her Latin book, her hair hanging limply over her eyes.

"Scarlet!" I hissed. No response. I tried poking her with my ink pen. Still no response.

I was about to give her a harder jab when, unfortunately, Miss Simons noticed. She paused mid-verb, walked over to Scarlet's desk and whacked the ruler down on the desk lid.

Scarlet sat bolt upright, hair still covering her face. "Mmm?" she said.

"Miss Grey! Do you find my lesson boring?"

Don't say it don't say it don't say it...

"Yes," said Scarlet, and put her face back down on her book.

Miss Simons' lower lip trembled and her cheeks flushed. "How dare you!"

Scarlet yawned, barely attempting to stifle it. "It's *utterly* dull, Miss. Can't we do something more fun?"

I shook my head frantically at my twin, but she wasn't looking at me, seemingly in a sleepy daze. Had she been out of the room again last night?

The teacher was fuming. "Miss Grey, Latin is a beautiful and important language, and I demand that you show it some respect!"

"I don't know any Romans," said Scarlet, "so why do I need to learn it?"

Giggles spread around the class.

"That's IT, young lady! Out!" The teacher thrust her ruler towards the door.

Scarlet climbed sluggishly to her feet and, without even remembering to pick up her satchel, walked out of the classroom. The door swung shut behind her.

"And you!" Miss Simons barked.

I looked around, wondering who she was talking to. And then as I turned back to the front, realisation dawned.

"Me?" I asked, puzzled.

"Yes, you! The other one!" She brandished the ruler at me.

What on earth? I hadn't done anything wrong. "I was

just... writing down the conjugations," I said quietly.

"Don't you try that with me! I'm not having both of you get away with insolence in my class!" She sounded panicked now, as if convinced I was about to instigate some kind of havoc.

"Miss, I didn't—" I protested.

"You can stand outside too – out!"

Not wanting to get in further trouble, I decided my best bet was to go along with it. I picked up my satchel – and Scarlet's – and walked out of the room. Ariadne looked at me in concern, and I shrugged.

Scarlet was standing outside in the corridor, leaning against the wall. She still looked half-asleep.

"What did *you* do?" she asked, squinting at me.

"Found guilty of being your twin," I said grumpily. I shoved her satchel back into her arms.

Scarlet smirked. "So you didn't do anything? Funny that. People getting accused of things they didn't do."

I gave her my best unimpressed face. "Shut up, Scarlet. We're both in trouble now."

"I won't be for much longer," she replied. But before I could ask what she meant, she'd grabbed my wrist.

I followed her gaze down the corridor. Someone was approaching.

The headmaster.

"You two," he said, pointing. His voice was quiet but heavy as lead as he shuffled closer. "Have you been sent out of class?" The anger in his eyes frightened me.

I wanted to say something, maybe even a witty retort. But now that Scarlet was back with me, I felt like I was shrinking again.

"No," said Scarlet.

I gave her a sideways glance. *What was she playing at?*

"I felt unwell," she said. "I've come out to get some air. And Miss sent Ivy to see if I was all right."

I blinked, surprised at how easily she lied. Then again, I had spent most of the past few months lying, hadn't I, when I was pretending to be her? I was in no position to judge.

Mr Bartholomew held Scarlet's gaze, locking her in some sort of staring contest. Trying to see if she would flinch. But I knew from experience that my twin wasn't easily cowed.

"Well," he said, finally, after what seemed like an age, "I hope I won't hear about any trouble where you're concerned. Things may have been... *lenient* around here in the past. But no longer." He took a few steps away from us.

Lenient? Under Miss Fox? I leant back against the wall, hoping it would swallow me up before I caught his attention.

"There'll be no trouble from me, sir," Scarlet said.

He looked back at her. "I know you, Scarlet Grey. I know your history. I know there are accusations of stealing against you already."

She pouted at him. "They were made up. I'm not a thief!"

"Nevertheless, young lady, you are on very. Thin. Ice."

He glared at us before stalking away. My heart was thumping and I felt like I was glued to the wall. But when I looked over at Scarlet, she was smiling.

"Did you see his face?" she said with a laugh. "What a nasty old bull! Ha! And *you* looked terrified!"

I bit my lip, feeling the anger rising in me.

"If you sank any further into that wall you'd be back in the classroom," she jibed.

"Shut up, Scarlet!" I yelled, making her jump. "We could get a caning, or worse, and it's all your fault! Can't you just *behave* for once?"

She frowned back at me. "Keep your voice down if you're so worried about getting told off, Miss Goody Two-Shoes."

"I just don't want to be punished for something I didn't even do!"

"Well, that makes two of us!"

"And you're *sure* you didn't steal those things?"

She gasped. I'd challenged her. "You know," she said finally, "I liked the *old* Ivy a lot better than this new argumentative one."

"At least some of us *have* changed and aren't just the same old nuisance we always were—"

"GIRLS!" It was Miss Simons. She'd flung the door open, her long hair whipping out behind her. "I will have silence when you're standing out here!"

She got silence.

A very angry, bitter silence.

I had spent so long wishing Scarlet was back in my life – and now she was, things were terrible between us.

A thought crossed my mind, a thought so awful I wanted to reject it immediately, but it stayed there, burned across my mind...

Was having my twin back really worth it, when she was nothing but trouble?

Chapter Nine

SCARLET

I had to clear my name.

As much as I hated to admit it, I *was* scared of Mr Bartholomew, as scared as I was of Miss Fox. I knew what Miss Fox was capable of, but the headmaster was a mystery.

And even more than that, I had to stop Ivy from hating me.

I *hadn't* stolen Penny's clothes or the food from the kitchens or the books. And I was going to prove it. I was going to creep around the school that night and try to catch the real thief red-handed.

Ivy finally went to sleep after an entire day of ignoring me, so I seized my chance. It took me a few minutes of standing by the door to build up the courage to open it. With a wrench of the handle it swung open, and I stared into what seemed like endless dark.

Don't be such a baby, I told myself. *There's nothing out there.*

As my eyes adjusted to the darkness, I forced myself to walk out to the stairs. I only had to take it one step at a time. There was nothing to be afraid of.

I passed a clock in the hall that told me it was nearly midnight. I caught my breath. The stairs were so close now. When I finally reached them, it felt like a triumph.

I can do this. I'll prove them all wrong.

As I tiptoed around the sleeping school, my confidence growing, the first place I thought to try was the kitchen. I crossed the dining hall, feet tapping on the wooden floor, until I reached the entrance.

Someone had added a handwritten sign that read 'COOKS AND DINNER LADIES ONLY. KEEP OUT'. I rolled my eyes. As if the thief would be deterred by a sign!

I tried the handle. *Locked.*

I put an ear to the door. I thought I could hear... something. There were muffled noises coming from inside. *Probably just mice*, I thought, but I sped away quickly.

I had to keep going. But where next? It was bitterly cold and goose bumps rose on my arms even with my coat pulled around me.

Perhaps the library?

I returned through the huge wooden doors and went back along the corridor towards the east wing of the school. I peered into the dark classrooms, finding them reassuringly empty. And I shuffled silently past Mr Bartholomew's office, my back to the wall.

The lights were on in the library.

It had a warm, inviting glow, but lights meant people. I poked my head round the doorway and had a look. *Nothing.* The place was empty but for the towering stacks of books.

Ivy had always loved storybooks, but I'd never had much time for them. Storybooks told you that you'd marry the handsome prince and live in a glorious castle. When really your evil stepmother sends you to live with a wicked witch who locks you away in a dungeon...

Happily ever afters don't *exist*.

I stepped into the room and walked over to the front desk to begin my search.

Or at least, that's what I intended to do. But at that moment someone leapt out from behind the desk, wielding a heavy book and yelling, "STAY BACK, I'M ARMED!"

I screamed.

And then I clamped my hand over my mouth, just as the librarian did the same.

"Oh gosh," she said to herself, setting the book down with a *thump*, "it's just a student. Just a student, Cassie." She paused and looked down at me. "You aren't a ghost, are you?"

"No, Miss," I said, my heart pounding. "Pretty certain I'm not."

"Thank goodness for that. I'm so sorry. I... goodness." She sat down on the wheeled wooden chair behind the desk and absent-mindedly brushed some dust off the book (*Flora and Fauna of Western Europe*).

When I'd got my breath back, I had to ask her the obvious question. "What are you doing here at this time of night, Miss?" *Though she could ask the exact same thing of me*, I realised.

The librarian was a slim woman dressed all in black, with dark hair cut in a tight bob with a straight fringe. She wore a name badge pinned to her dress that read 'C. Jones', and blinked at me for a moment before answering. "Protecting the books," she said.

I nodded slowly, thinking she might be a *bit* mad.

"Do I know you?" she said suddenly.

"I don't think so. I've not been in here much." I realised

that I had to keep talking, because she hadn't yet thought to ask me what *I* was doing in there. "You might have seen my twin?"

"Oh! Twin! That might be it, perhaps."

"Miss... What are you protecting the books *from*?"

She stared at me with wide eyes, and then lowered her voice, despite there being no one around. "I think there's a ghost."

Maybe she was more than a bit mad. "You think a ghost stole the books?"

The librarian stood up again and silently beckoned for me to follow her. She led me through the stacks and over to a dimly lit area of the library that smelt of musty old paper, our footsteps echoing in the vast empty room. This particular corner seemed a little abandoned, and hadn't seen much interest in some time. The books that lined the shelves were old and tattered; they looked as though they would crumble to pieces if you touched them.

She pointed at the floor, and I followed her finger with my gaze.

There were dusty footprints going *into* the bookcase.

I knelt down and stared at them, wondering what I was seeing. The small footprints led towards the bottom shelf and then stopped halfway through, a lone heel disappearing into them. *As if someone had walked right through.*

Miss Jones was looking around nervously, and I didn't blame her, because for a moment a shiver passed through me.

No, I was being foolish. There was no such thing as ghosts.

I put my own foot against the prints – they were roughly the same size. "It is very strange, Miss," I said. I reminded myself why I was there – I needed to find out who was really behind this if I was going to clear my name. "Did you see anything? Hear anything?"

She frowned, thinking. "I haven't seen anyone go over to this part of the library. But I have been hearing things. It's not just these footprints and the books being stolen, there've been sounds too. Strange noises in the walls. Sometimes I think I can hear *voices*."

Sometimes, so can I.

I straightened up and peered at one of the stacks. "Which books were stolen, exactly?"

Miss Jones gave a little sniff. She was clearly emotional about these things. "They were storybooks, mainly. Beatrix Potter. E.E. Nesbit. *Peter Pan* and *The Secret Garden*. I was proud of those. Lovely editions. Oh, and books about ponies."

I thought about it. So whoever (or whatever) had been here had taken books and had feet a similar size to mine. And they may or may not have been able to walk through walls. Well, that was a start.

"I'm just so frightened," she continued, "but I don't want anything else to be taken. This is all I've got, you know." She gestured at the towering shelves of the library.

I reached up and gave her a sympathetic pat on the shoulder. "You'll be fine, Miss. I just need to figure this out. They –" I stopped, unsure whether to confide in her, but something told me to carry on – "they think that it was me who's been stealing things, but it wasn't, I swear! I need to find out who did this, ghost or no ghost."

She smiled then, a worried smile, but her eyes shone and crinkled at the corners. "Well, I wish you the best of luck. I was beginning to consider calling a priest to exorcise the room, but if you can find out what's going on here..."

"I will." It was a promise.

We stood without saying anything for a moment. I listened. There was nothing, save for a quiet rustling in the distance and the occasional creak as the old building settled.

Miss Jones broke the silence. "Thank you for keeping me company," she said. "I suppose you shouldn't really be in here at night, but then I shouldn't, either. It was nice to meet you..."

"Scarlet."

"Nice to meet you, Scarlet. I'm Catastrophe Jones."

I stared, not sure if I'd heard her properly. "Catastrophe? As in... an awful event?"

"Yes," she sighed. "My mother came from China, and she had a passion for unusual English words. I usually go by Cassie instead." She looked down at her watch, a dainty, pretty one that hung from her wrist. "Goodness, it's late. Run along now, my dear, or you'll get into trouble."

She was right. But at least I was that tiny bit closer to figuring out who was responsible for all this. I had one last question, though, as I looked at the heavy book on her desk. "Miss, how exactly were you going to hit a ghost? Don't things pass straight through them?"

The librarian suddenly went very pale. "I didn't think of that," she said.

Chapter Ten

Ivy

I had tried to stay awake to keep an eye on Scarlet, but I hadn't managed it. And now it was breakfast time, and Scarlet was so sleepy I thought she was about to doze off in her porridge. I wanted to believe that she'd just had a restless night, but my instincts told me that she'd been off somewhere again. *Stealing?*

I chastised myself for thinking that. Though I was cross with my twin for being so secretive, she had sworn to me that she wasn't the thief. She may have been a troublemaker, but she'd not given me any reason to believe she would lie to me. At least, not since we had been reunited...

Ariadne was watching Penny write in her prefect book. "She's almost filled the whole book! That's a lot of apparently suspicious behaviour," she said.

Ethel Hadlow nudged Penny when she saw us staring. Penny just glared and made a show of writing something down.

"What?" I said to Ariadne. "They're going to report us for *looking* at them?" But then again, it *was* Penny. I wasn't exactly surprised. At least Nadia was friendly with us now. She gave us a surreptitious wave from down the table.

Ariadne turned to Scarlet. "Have *you* seen anything suspicious? What with the thefts and all?"

Scarlet frowned at her, and I wondered if she thought she was being accused again. "Possibly a ghost," she said.

We both went wide-eyed.

"I'm serious," she continued. "Well, I'm not sure if I believe it's a ghost, but something weird is going on, anyway. I went to the library..."

"*You* went to the library?" I couldn't believe what I was hearing.

"That is beside the point. The point is that not only have some of the books gone missing, but there were footprints going *into the wall*. And the librarian said she's been hearing strange noises. She seemed terrified."

"A ghost," said Ariadne. "Goodness. Well, that would explain a lot, wouldn't it? Like how they're getting in everywhere, and why they haven't been caught yet."

"It might explain a lot if ghosts were real," Scarlet replied, nonchalantly eating another spoonful of porridge. "Which they're not."

"But if they were," Ariadne continued. "Who would it be? No one's died here, have they?"

Nadia stopped right behind us with her tray, the empty bowl sliding to the edge. "You don't know about the girl who died?"

We all shook our heads.

She glanced quickly at Mrs Knight, who thankfully wasn't paying attention, and leant down beside the table. "I heard that, about twenty years ago, there was some sort of accident. Something went terribly wrong, and a girl drowned."

I looked at my twin and saw my own horror reflected in her face. "Really?"

Nadia shrugged. "It might just be a rumour. But apparently there's a memorial plaque somewhere. Penny and I went looking for it, but we couldn't find anything."

"P-perhaps it's just something they make up to scare first years," Ariadne said hopefully.

"Who knows," Nadia replied. "But just in case, you must watch out for the water." She gave a wink, stood back up and walked away.

The thought gave me goose bumps. Nadia had pushed me into the pool not long ago, and I'd almost drowned. She may have been under the impression that I was Scarlet, but still. Thank goodness she'd dropped her vendetta after finding out about Miss Fox locking my sister away in the asylum.

"Well, that was creepy—" I started, but I could tell Ariadne's brain was already whirring.

"We need to look into this," she said. "If Scarlet isn't the thief, then we've got to find out who is. Even if it's a ghost."

She had a point.

"What do you mean, *if* I'm not the thief?" Scarlet demanded, before brightening up. "Then you'll help me?" she said.

"Of course," me and Ariadne chorused, but I felt bad that I was just a moment behind.

Throughout that day's sermon in the chapel, all I could think about was the ghost. Or more specifically, the girl who had died. I wondered if she was buried in the little overgrown graveyard outside, if the plaque to her was one of those that peppered the walls.

It was unlikely, though. The chapel was old, and I'd not seen a date any later than 1880 on any of the memorials.

Perhaps Nadia had just been trying to frighten us a little.

But as I sat shivering in the cold, wrapping my cardigan tighter around me, I looked at my twin sitting next to me. And I remembered what had happened to her.

Scary things *did* happen at this school. Things that the teachers seemed very keen to cover up...

We had free time that afternoon, and that meant investigating – Ariadne was nothing if not determined.

"Can you show us what you found in the library, Scarlet?" she asked.

Scarlet leant over to me. "Does she *have* to tag along?" she said in a stage whisper. I glared at her, but Ariadne didn't seem deflated.

We trekked over to the east wing. When we got there, Violet was sitting by herself at one of the tables. She was studying, writing things down in a jotter with books open all around her.

"I just don't get it," said Ariadne. "She's completely silent the whole time she's in our room. I thought she'd at least be a *bit* mean to me. I don't think she even talks to her old friends."

It was strange, that was certain. Was Violet's withdrawn manner because of whatever had happened to her? And if so, was Scarlet equally broken? I looked at my twin, but her expression gave nothing away. She just seemed like the same old Scarlet.

"Forget Violet," she said. "Let's find Miss Jones."

Ariadne and I followed Scarlet through the stacks. It was fairly busy at this time of day, many bustling girls with arms full of books, chatting in hushed voices.

We found the librarian staring at one of the bookshelves.

"Um, Miss?" asked Ariadne.

Miss Jones turned around, fiddling with her name tag. "Hmm?"

"What are you looking at?" asked Scarlet.

The librarian pointed at the dusty shelves. "There's something not right here," she said. "I haven't got round to cataloguing this bit yet, but I'm sure these books are... different."

"Different how?" I asked, peering around her.

"The spines don't look right. And these titles..." She shook her head, as if trying and failing to dislodge the right information. "Sorry, girls. Did you want to speak to me? And goodness – don't you two look alike!"

"We came about the G-H-O-S-T," Ariadne spelt out.

Miss Jones went pale. "Oh yes. I'm afraid there's nothing else to report. But you're welcome to have a look around, if you like. I'll be at the desk." She scuttled away, leaving us looking confused.

"The footprints have gone," Scarlet pointed out, after a

moment of silence.

Ariadne bent down and examined the bottom of the shelf. She touched an inquisitive finger to the floor. "There's water here," she said, crinkling her nose.

Water. Like the girl who drowned.

I didn't say that aloud. It seemed silly.

"Maybe the caretaker mopped the floor. Or the culprit tried to get rid of the prints," my twin suggested.

I nodded. But my mind wouldn't stop picturing the ghost, gliding through the air in wet rags, hair streaming out behind her, as though she was trapped by weeds underwater.

I turned round, and Violet was right in front of me.

"Stay away," she hissed.

I nearly screamed, but I managed to stop myself. Violet may not have been a ghost, but she had appeared suddenly and her eyes were wild. Not to mention that they were the first words I'd ever heard her speak.

"Stay away from what?" asked my twin, stepping between us.

Violet's eyes darted back and forth and she appeared disgusted that she had another Grey to deal with. "From here," she hissed again. "Just stop whatever you're doing. *Stop it.*"

Before Scarlet could open her mouth to argue, Violet had already turned and stalked away.

Chapter Eleven

SCARLET

"She's the ghost!" said Ariadne.

"She's the *thief*!" I slapped my palm against my forehead. "Of course! We were getting close to catching her, so now she's making threats. Why else would she suddenly remember how to talk just to tell us to stay away?"

My twin looked pensive. "That makes sense, I suppose. But how can we prove it? Everyone knows you and Violet hate each other, I don't think accusing her is going to get you very far."

She had a point. But I had an idea.

"Just you wait," I said.

That night, I considered telling Ivy that I was going to slip out of the room and investigate again. I wanted to catch Violet prowling around after lights out and confirm that she was behind the spate of thefts. But I knew my twin would just try to talk me out of it, say that I was going to get myself in more trouble. And I'd only just managed to get her to start speaking to me again... it was best to keep this latest excursion a secret for now.

I can handle trouble, I thought to myself. *Trouble is practically my middle name.*

As I waited, I watched the frost climbing the glass, listening to Ivy's gentle snoring, and feeling the crisp bed sheets against my skin. I was so tired, perhaps I should just stay in bed... but then there was a harsh, clanking noise from the walls, and I jumped right up.

It was just the heating pipes, I knew that. That was all it was.

I took a deep breath, and walked out of room thirteen and into the darkness.

I moved along the corridor until I came to room twenty-four, where Ariadne and Violet would be sleeping. I supposed I could have asked Ariadne to spy on Violet, but I didn't quite trust her yet. And besides, Ivy had told me that Ariadne usually slept like a log – or maybe even a whole tree.

Their dorm was at the end of a corridor, just around the corner from the lavatories. So I sat down, hopefully out of sight, and I watched.

After about ten minutes, I began to wonder if it was a stupid idea. I could sit out in the corridor all night and freeze to death.

After half an hour, and the loss of sensation in my toes and fingertips, I was *certain* it was a stupid idea.

But that was when I heard the school's big grandfather clock chime midnight. And then came a creak, and the door of room twenty-four began to open.

I dodged into the lavatories and leant back against the cold wall, my heart racing. Violet had better not have got up just to go to the toilet.

I slowed my breathing down and ordered my heartbeat to calm itself. And then I heard the footsteps go past the door. *Time to go.*

Tiptoeing back out, I spied Violet heading for the stairs. I almost shouted at her impulsively, wanting to tell her she was caught, wanting to see the look on her face. But I stopped myself. *Stupid.* I had no proof that she'd done anything yet.

I followed quickly and quietly, straining to see if she was still ahead of me in the darkness. I could hear the swishing of her nightgown as she hurried, until suddenly she stopped dead and whipped round to look behind her.

I snapped my head back and plastered myself against the wall, trying to hold my breath. Had she seen me?

I listened. Silence. I waited.

That has to be long enough. I looked back, heart pounding, just in time to see her ebony hair and white nightdress slipping around the corner. I was safe. But where was she going?

I sped up, not wanting to lose her. It wasn't long before I realised the answer was obvious: *the library.* She was returning to the scene of one of the crimes. Maybe she was going to steal some more books. This was going to be *good.* I hoped Miss Jones would be there too, to witness me triumphantly unmasking Violet as the thief and clearing my name.

Contrary to my suspicions, all the lights but one were switched off in the library, leaving a dim orange glow, and there were no obvious signs of life. If Miss Jones had been there, she wasn't now.

Violet had slowed down as she walked into the vast room, and I watched her as she approached the desk cautiously, probably checking for ambushing librarians. She walked around it, and I saw her picking through some of Miss Jones's papers and books. There was nothing Violet liked better than spying, though you'd have thought that the fact her snooping about in Miss Fox's desk drawer led to her disappearance would have taught her a lesson.

Of course, *I* wasn't spying. I was catching a criminal. That was different.

Violet walked off in the direction of the stacks where we'd found the footprints – and that was my cue to follow. I sneaked behind her, between the towering bookshelves. I approached the dark corner, coiled like a spring, poised to catch her in the act...

But she was gone.

I stopped still. Where on *earth* was she? She'd been right in front of me!

I turned round slowly, panic rising. If Violet jumped out at me, there was no telling what she'd do. Scenes of the rooftop flashed into my mind, the cold and the dark flooding in, and I fought the urge to whimper.

Calm down, I told myself. *Keep looking.*

So I searched, pacing the stacks, struggling not to cough in the dusty air, anticipating that at any moment I'd come face to face with my worst enemy. But it didn't happen.

Violet had well and truly disappeared.

Suddenly, I became aware of how alone I was. Alone, in the dark, in the enormous library, that may or may not have been haunted, in deathly silence.

No, not silence.

There was a distant creaking, heavy thuds below my feet, the sound of the wind howling in the trees.

And there were whispers in the walls.

I ran.

Chapter Twelve

IVY

carlet shook me awake in the middle of the night.

"What?" I murmured groggily, sitting up. I could just make out my twin's panicked face. "What is it?"

"I followed Violet."

"You did *what*?"

Scarlet sat down on my bed, her breathing ragged as if she'd been running. "I thought I'd catch her stealing, so I could prove it wasn't me." She paused and gulped a breath of air. "So I waited outside her room until she came out. She

went all the way down to the library, and then she, she..."
Another pause. "She disappeared."

I was awake now. I wrapped the covers around myself, trying to keep out the chilly night air. "What do you mean, 'she disappeared'?" It wasn't as if this was the first time that Violet had gone missing.

"One minute she was walking off through the shelves, then she was gone. And I don't have a clue where. And I heard voices. I think."

Now this was strange. I thought I should probably give Scarlet a good talking-to for chasing after Violet, especially without me, but it sounded like whatever was going on was more curious than I'd ever imagined.

I had a horrible thought. "W-what if it wasn't Violet that you saw? What if it was the ghost?"

"Ivy," she said, and although I couldn't see very clearly in the dark, I could tell from Scarlet's tone of voice that she had probably rolled her eyes. "I really doubt it. Unless the ghost has been sleeping in Ariadne's room without her noticing."

I lay back down in bed, suppressing a shiver that I told myself was just the cold. "We need sleep. Well, I need sleep, at least. We can tell Ariadne about this tomorrow, and see if she's got any ideas about what happened. She's usually good at figuring these things out."

Scarlet huffed at this. "I don't see why we need to wait for your *friend*! Let's go and investigate now, ̶

But I stood up to her. "No, Scarlet̶
sneaking around, we'll be punished by M̶
I don't want to get in trouble again! We wait un̶

Scarlet look dumbfounded at my words, but stood up and crossed the room, slipping under her covers as if she'd never been gone. And then, after a few moments of silence, she said, "Can we trust her?"

"Ariadne?" The idea of someone *not* trusting her was perplexing to me.

"Yes. It's not like you've known her for long. And now she shares a room with Violet."

"That doesn't mean anything. She's still the same person. And you wouldn't even be here if it wasn't for her – she helped me track down the pages of your diary!"

Scarlet went quiet again.

When it became clear she wasn't going to say any more, my eyes drifted shut, and I fell back into the sleep I'd been so rudely awakened from.

Ghosts and disappearing girls could wait for tomorrow.

I was desperate to get down to breakfast and tell Ariadne what had happened, despite Scarlet's misgivings.

I looked over at the Evergreen table when we arrived, but there was no sign of Violet. Ariadne was already at our table, utinising her porridge. We sat down, and I filled her in on the previous night's events.

"Violet *disappeared*?" she said, eyes wide. "*Again?*"

"Well, I'm pretty sure Miss Fox wasn't involved this time," Scarlet replied sarcastically. "This was a whole different kind of disappearing."

"And you're certain there was no one else in the library?"

"Of course! I looked everywhere. Nobody. She was there and then a few seconds later she was gone." Scarlet leant back in her chair, tipping it so far I thought she was going to fall over. "Explain that one."

Ariadne's eyebrows knitted in puzzlement. "Okay, well, I can't. Not without finding out more. All I know is that she was back in her bed this morning. I asked her if she was coming down for breakfast and she just grunted at me."

We all sat in silence for a moment, considering it.

"Oh," said Ariadne, "but I did notice that she had some library books poking out of her satchel. They could be the missing ones – the classics and pony stories. But why would she be stealing books when she could just borrow them? It doesn't make any sense…"

Mrs Knight walked up behind Scarlet and pushed her chair upright again. "Miss Grey, do you want to do yourself an injury?"

My twin didn't answer, and instead just picked up her

spoon and gobbled a mouthful of her porridge.

Mrs Knight frowned and sat down in her seat. "Goodness, didn't your mother teach you any manners?"

"My mother is dead," said Scarlet loudly, and carried on eating.

My mouth fell open in horror, and the whole of the Richmond table went silent.

"Well, really!" Mrs Knight managed eventually.

Lots of the other pupils were staring at us, and I felt my cheeks flush red. I thought of kicking Scarlet under the table, but it was too late. The damage was done.

She seemed oblivious. "What are you looking at?" she yelled at everyone. Even Penny looked taken aback.

"Scarlet Grey," said Mrs Knight, "you are *excused*! Don't come back until you've learnt how to talk to your betters!"

Scarlet slammed down the spoon and stormed off.

Now everyone turned their stares to *me*. I gave a weak smile, thinking life at Rookwood had definitely been less embarrassing without Scarlet around. Why did she have to be so hot-headed?

That was not the only time my sister caused trouble that day. She seemed to be on a mission to annoy every teacher in the school.

We sat in physics on the tall stools behind the heavy block

desks. Miss Danver had let Scarlet and I sit together in her lessons. There was a slight problem with this: the rather scatter-brained teacher couldn't tell us apart. Whenever I put up my hand to answer a question, she called me Scarlet. At first I forgot to correct her – I'd become so used to having to answer to my twin's name.

"Ivy," she asked at one point, "could you go and get the wires from the cupboard, please?" We were supposed to be making electric bell circuits.

I stood up.

"No, not you. Ivy," she said, pointing a thin finger at Scarlet.

"I'm Ivy, Miss," I pointed out, as Scarlet snickered.

"Oh." She put a hand to her mouth, momentarily puzzled. "Well, then. Scarlet, can you go, please."

She then began chalking up the electric diagram on the board. Scarlet headed for the supplies cupboard at the back of the room.

A loud bang and a worrying whooshing sound shortly followed.

Miss Danver frowned. "Penny, will you go and see what Scarlet's getting up to in there?"

I shot a look at Ariadne, who sat a few seats away beside the silent Violet. Ariadne shrugged.

As a triumphant-looking Penny got up from the back

of the class and went in, I watched, frozen, awaiting the inevitable.

"Ah! Scarlet! What *are* you doing? Miss! She's got water everywhere!" As Penny spoke, a trickle of water pooled out on to the floor.

"Turn that tap off right now!" the physics teacher shouted.

"It's stuck!" I heard Scarlet yell back. I fought the urge to slam my head on the desk. Why had she turned on the tap?

Miss Danver put her hands on her hips and headed in, struggling with the tap before managing to turn it off. She then emerged, pulling Scarlet by the arm. The bottom of her long dress was soaked. "Scarlet Grey," she said, "why exactly did you think 'go and get the wires' meant 'go and flood the place'?"

My twin narrowed her eyes. "Well, I didn't mean to do that, *obviously*," she said.

Our teacher's face was red and her nostrils flared. "Water and electricity should not mix, young lady. Get out of my classroom. You can come back at three o'clock for detention!"

"But Miss—" said Scarlet.

"Out!"

"I'm writing this down in my book, Miss," said Penny haughtily, despite no one asking her. She adjusted her blue hair bow that had gone askew and pulled out the prefect notebook from her pocket. "Well done, *Scarlet.*"

Scarlet grabbed the notebook from her and tossed it to the floor. Then she stalked out of the room, leaving Miss Danver open-mouthed.

I put my head in my hands. My twin and I may look identical, but sometimes I wondered how we could even be related.

"I can't have detention," said Scarlet, as if not believing it would make it not true.

"Of course you blooming well can. You behaved like an idiot."

"No, I mean, I can't do it. I have to keep Violet under constant surveillance. Ariadne saw books in her satchel, and I reckon they're the stolen ones. She must be going to return them! I could follow her and see whether they're the ones that went missing. How am I going to do that if I'm stuck in the physics classroom?"

We were walking down the corridor for the last lesson of the day: ballet.

"You're not. There's your answer. Why were you messing with the taps, anyway?"

"I was thirsty." Scarlet shrugged. "I just turned the tap on for a second, and then I got distracted thinking about the water that we found under the bookshelf. And then when I tried to turn it off, the stupid thing got stuck."

I sighed. Trust Scarlet to find new ways of getting into trouble.

Suddenly, my twin pushed me back out of the flow of girls moving between classrooms and into an alcove. "I've had an idea," she whispered.

Oh no, not again. "What is it this time?"

"You take my place. At detention."

"Scarlet, no—"

She looked around, making sure no one was listening. "Miss Danver can't tell us apart anyway. It's a brilliant idea."

"No, it's a terrible idea." I tried to carry on walking, worried we'd be late for ballet, but she pulled on my arm so I couldn't go any further.

"If you take my detention for me, I can find out what Violet's up to."

"Why can't *I* find out what she's up to?" I asked.

"Because if someone's going to confront her, it's going to be me. I'm the one who stands to get in much bigger trouble here if Penny gets any more evidence on me! And besides, are you really going to have the guts to stand up to Violet?"

I gaped at her. I'd stood up to Miss Fox, hadn't I? Did that mean nothing?

"Well, that's settled," Scarlet said. "You go to the

detention, I'll keep an eye on Violet."

Before I could even argue, she was darting away through the crowds.

So at three o'clock, I was back in the physics classroom.

Miss Danver looked up from her desk, where she was marking work. "Ah, Scarlet," she said. "Come in and sit down. One hundred lines of 'I must do as I'm told', please."

"Yes, Miss," I replied despondently, taking a seat and a piece of paper.

"You were doing so well these past few months. It's been like having a different person in my lessons! I thought you'd turned over a new leaf."

I sighed. "So did I."

I had barely written five lines when there was a knock at the door. I looked up at the teacher and, to my surprise, the colour had drained from her face.

"Come in," she said.

It was Mr Bartholomew.

I held my breath, stared down at the piece of paper and tried to pretend I wasn't there. It was no use. He'd spotted me.

"Grey," he said, his voice flat and cold.

I looked up slowly. "Sir?"

But his attention had already shifted back to Miss Danver,

and he leant over her desk, his palms flat on the surface. "This child has misbehaved," he said, like it was a statement, rather than a question.

"Yes, sir," she replied, her voice quivering.

There was a moment of painful silence. "And do you think that writing lines will dissuade her from doing so again?"

"I... well, it's—"

"It will not," he said. "*Creative punishment.* I want you to remember those two words. Children are endlessly thinking of new ways to make trouble. We must stay one step ahead of them."

Just the sound of his horrible, throaty voice made me feel unwell. I blinked at my five lines and they began to swim in front of my eyes.

"What was the offence?" he continued.

"S-she nearly flooded the classroom," Miss Danver said. "She shouldn't have been touching the taps."

For what seemed like forever there was no sound but the headmaster's rasping breaths. He stared out of the window at the dark sky, where the morning's misty drizzle had turned into an afternoon downpour.

"Yes," he said, apparently coming to a conclusion. "Yes, that should do it." He still wasn't looking at me. "Four laps of the school, in the rain. That should teach her to play with water. I'll be watching."

My brain was tying itself in knots. Should I be Scarlet, and tell him he must be mad if he thought I was going to do that? Should I be Ivy and dutifully accept my punishment with no more than a 'yes, sir'?

As Mr Bartholomew shuffled out of the room, I looked at Miss Danver imploringly. "Right now?" I asked.

Miss Danver shook her head as if mentally brushing herself off, and then regained her authority. "You heard the headmaster. Chop chop!"

I dragged myself to my feet and out into the corridor. As I walked along, I silently cursed my sister with every step.

This is all your fault, Scarlet.

I can't believe I'm doing this.

I came to one of the back doors of the school to find it held open by Mr Bartholomew, a sneer on his wrinkled face. The punishment he would give me if I dared to disobey was too terrible to contemplate.

I took a deep breath, and I stepped out into the driving rain.

Chapter Thirteen

SCARLET

I felt a little bad for making Ivy take my detention, but it was definitely a load off my mind. I sailed through ballet, managing a nearly perfect *tour jeté*. I was absolutely determined to keep Violet in my sights for the rest of the day.

I hadn't intended to take Ariadne with me, but I bumped into her as she returned from hockey.

"Oh, Scarlet," she said. She squinted for a moment. "Scarlet? It is you, isn't it? It's harder to tell you apart when you're not standing next to each other."

Well, I *was* going to agree with her. I definitely was. But then I realised I could have some fun with this. "No, it's me, Ivy," I said. "Scarlet's got detention, remember?"

"Sorry!" she said, whacking her hand on to her forehead. "I'm such an idiot. So where are you going?"

"I'm tracking Violet. It looks like she's heading to the library."

"Right! I'll come too."

Ariadne followed, telling me every excruciating detail of what had just happened in her hockey lesson.

"...and then Clara hit the ball so hard that it ended up in the tree, and Mrs Briggs spent the rest of the lesson perched on a ladder, trying to knock it down with a stick."

I nodded my way through the story, listening politely. I figured that's what Ivy would do.

We walked into the library, and almost crashed into Miss Jones, who was wheeling a trolley full of books.

"Oh! Hello, girls," she said, yawning. "Sorry, I didn't see you there." She leant down towards me over the trolley. "I couldn't stay here last night," she said in a lowered voice. "Mrs Knight caught me and said it was inappropriate to be hanging around after lights out." She sighed. "I came in early this morning. No sign of the ghost, but... I swear the books on that shelf were different again. I'm telling you, someone's been messing around with them."

"Can ghosts move books?" Ariadne asked, sounding a little frightened.

"I don't know," Miss Jones replied. "Maybe. It could be a poltergeist. One of those angry spirits that flings things about. But who knows – everything still seems neatly arranged. I almost wonder if I should report this to the headmaster."

The last thing we needed was *him* getting any more involved. "*We'll* help you find the culprit, Miss."

"Thank you," she said absent-mindedly, before bustling off into the stacks with the trolley.

The library clock quietly chimed three times, and we spotted Violet approaching the front desk.

I marched over to her. "Hey, Violet!"

She was wearing her satchel, and I could see the books peeking out of it. *Now's my chance to prove these are the stolen books!*

"Gotcha!" I tugged on her bag, hard, and the contents came spilling out.

Oh.

They were just physics textbooks.

"I was *returning* them," said Violet quietly, and her dark eyes burned into mine with such intensity that the hairs on the back of my neck stood up. "Why can't you just leave me alone? Haven't you done enough?"

She gathered the books up from the floor and dropped the whole pile on to Miss Jones's desk. Then she walked off angrily, her bag swaying as she went.

"Scarlet?"

I turned around. Ariadne was looking up at me. She didn't seem happy. *Rats.*

"You shouldn't have done that, Scarlet."

"What? I had to know."

"Ivy would never act like that. You shouldn't have lied to me."

"Oh. Well, sorry." I changed the subject quickly. "But I think we've rattled Violet! I bet she'll be back here later tonight, she's definitely up to *something.* But this time we won't wait until she sneaks out of your room. We'll be in here already – and catch her in the act!"

Ariadne had been looking sulky, but her eyes lit up at this plan. "Let's report back to Ivy!" she said.

I went back to our dorm, mind alight with thoughts of catching Violet.

As I sat down, Ivy walked in, and she was *soaked.* Her hair and clothes were dripping wet, and she was shivering.

"I hate you," she said to me. She picked up a threadbare towel from the chair and started rubbing her face with it.

"What? What have I done? And why are you so wet?"

"Mr Bartholomew was a special guest at *your* detention. He made me run round the school in the rain."

I raised my eyebrows. "Yikes. Glad I wasn't there, then."

She threw the towel at me. "You just don't get it, do you?" she yelled.

"Get what?" It was so strange to hear her talk like that, snapping at me. She usually just went along with everything I said and did.

"What I went through. I had to pretend to be you, for ages! And you've just made me do it again!"

I frowned. "We used to pretend to be each other all the time, or have you forgotten?"

"No, Scarlet," she said, and I couldn't tell whether her eyes were wet from rain or tears. "You'd say you were me, and then I'd get in trouble. There was no 'we' about it. It was always you. And then you were gone, and I had to..."

There was definitely a sob there. I started to feel a bit sick.

I'd been so annoyed with Ivy for doubting me, for making new friends, and I hadn't even stopped to think what she'd been through.

"I'm an idiot," I said.

Ivy's eyes narrowed. She was clearly wondering what I was getting at.

"I'm such a colossal idiot that you could probably see me from space." I gave her a (very damp) hug. "I won't do it again. And I'll make an effort to be more thoughtful. Forgive me?"

"I still hate you," she said. But she hugged me back.

Night fell, and it was time to hunt for Violet.

Ivy was still cross, but she insisted on coming with us. "I'm not letting you go alone," she said. "You'll just get into even more trouble."

Violet had left her room at the stroke of midnight the night before – I had heard the grandfather clock chime – so Ivy and I slipped out of our room at half past eleven. Ariadne met us in the corridor.

"I told Violet that I didn't feel well and was going to the sick bay to find Nurse Gladys. She won't be expecting me to come back," she whispered, eyes gleaming.

I smiled, impressed. "Well done, Ariadne. We'll make a good liar of you yet. Let's go!"

"It's freezing," said Ariadne, as we crept through the dark corridors of the school towards the library. I shushed her, and Ivy made a face at me.

We trekked through the stacks of books and over to the dark corner. Ariadne sat down against one of the shelves sleepily, while I paced up and down, ready to pounce should Violet appear. Ivy was staring at the books.

"Hmm," she said.

"What is it?"

"It's just... this is where the ghostly footprints were, right?"

"Yes."

"And it was around here that you saw Violet vanish?"

I nodded quickly, wanting her to get to the point.

"And Miss Jones says... she says the books keep changing?"

Ariadne suddenly shot to her feet, faster than I'd ever seen her move. "OH MY GOSH!" she cried in a loud whisper.

"What? What am I missing?"

Ariadne looked back and forth between us like an excited meerkat. "It's not a bookcase! It looks like a bookcase, but it's not! It's a door!"

I may have stood there open-mouthed for a second, staring at my sister and her friend, who were both grinning at me. But then I properly registered what they were getting at. Of course! *Of course!* "We have to open it!"

"If the books are changing," said Ariadne, holding up a finger, "then there must be books on the other side. *It swings round*. We need to push on one side."

That I could do. I took hold of one of the wooden shelves, dug my heels into the floor and pushed as hard as I could.

For a moment, nothing happened.

But then there was a click, and the whole creaking contraption swung sideways, leaving us looking into blackness.

I peered in. It was a small space, not much bigger than a cupboard, but there seemed to be... stairs?

Ivy had brought a candle stub, which she lit with a match and held out into the void. It was indeed stairs, a steep spiral descending into the ground. Her hand was shaking a little, and the candlelight sputtered and flicked odd shadows on to the wall.

"Come on," I whispered, grabbing her other hand and pulling her in.

Ariadne was still staring at the moving bookcase. "Fascinating," she muttered.

"You too, swot."

"Oh! Right! Yes..."

It was damp and cold in the stairwell. The steps were made of thick slabs of wood, and they looked old – I could make out rot and woodworm holes in the candlelight. Hopefully they would hold our weight. Our breathing and footsteps echoed off the walls as we moved.

I could feel the claustrophobia creeping in.

This is a trap. You need to escape. Miss Fox could be down here, waiting...

I slowed my breathing and gripped Ivy's hand tighter. As long as she was with me, everything would be okay. I wouldn't be trapped again.

"Who do you think built this?" Ariadne's whisper drifted down from behind me as I took another cautious step. "It must be from back when the school was a grand house."

"Shh," I replied with a finger to my lips. Just in case we really weren't alone, I didn't want anyone to know we were coming.

And then, suddenly, we were at the bottom.

And there was another door.

"A secret room," breathed Ariadne.

The door looked as old as the stairs, heavy and wooden with iron rivets and a huge metal handle. There was a thick bolt slid across it.

I let go of Ivy's hand and leant against a damp wall for a moment, dizzy, my fear threatening to overcome me. But we hadn't come this far to *not* go into a secret room. I had to know what was in there.

Slowly, quietly, I pulled back the rusty bolt.

Then I took a deep breath, and I opened the door.

Chapter Fourteen

Ivy

There was a girl inside the room.

She was sitting on the floor looking up at us, surrounded by burning candles, and there was a smile on her face.

She was as pale as a ghost.

I screamed.

It came out before I could even stop myself. I slammed my hands over my mouth, realising what I had just done. *If anyone heard me...*

The girl stood up, and moved towards us, still smiling.

Shaking, I backed away. I held the candle out in front of me as if it would protect me, somehow. I wanted to run. Scarlet's eyes were wide and Ariadne was staring in horror.

But then something happened: my twin held out her hand.

There was a moment where we all froze, fixated on what was happening. I dropped the candle to the floor. It fizzled out.

The girl took Scarlet's hand.

"She's real," Scarlet whispered, and all of the air rushed out of my lungs in relief. *Not a ghost. There's no such thing as ghosts.*

"H-hello?" said Ariadne, taking a step forward. The strange girl just nodded at her, still not talking.

I paused, trying to slow my heart back to its normal rate, and looked around the mysterious room. The girl had the most beautiful long blonde hair, I noticed, but it was bedraggled, and she was wearing a dress and jumper that looked a little too big. The room she sat in was bare but for the candles, a makeshift bed in the corner, an old trunk and...

"Scarlet," I said, pointing. "Look."

My sister took her eyes off the girl for a second and her eyes followed mine to the back wall.

"Oh my..."

The back wall of the room was illuminated by the dancing

orange candlelight, and above an old tapestry heaped on the floor, it was *full* of writing. The words crept all the way up to the ceiling.

"Did *she* do that?" asked Ariadne, grabbing my arm.

The girl just stared, and her eyes seemed cautious.

Part of me was desperate to look, but a bigger part of me was desperate to turn and run. "We need to get out of here," I said, tugging on Scarlet's sleeve. "We need to tell someone about this!"

But my twin wouldn't budge; she was rooted to the spot, taking in the words. Ariadne too was stock-still, dumbstruck.

This is all wrong, I thought. If I had to drag Scarlet out of there, I would. Who knew *who* or *what* this girl was...

And just as I was thinking that, she shot out her arm and pointed at me, and her eyes bored into me like she was reading my soul.

I couldn't stand a second more of this. I turned to run—

And smacked straight into Violet.

"No!" she cried out. "No, no NO! You're not supposed to... this is..."

I stumbled backwards. She backed up into the doorway, and before I could say anything, she'd collapsed in tears.

"V-Violet?" said Ariadne.

"*Violet?*" said Scarlet.

"Violet!" whispered the strange girl. We all turned to look

at her, not quite believing that she could actually talk.

Violet was still sobbing into her arms, but she soon lifted her head, and I saw that the familiar fire had returned. "What are you doing here?" she said, her voice shaking. "How could you. How *could* you?" She jumped to her feet and ran at Scarlet, pushing her back against the wall by the little folding bed. Ariadne gasped, while the ghost girl merely giggled.

"Get away from me!" Scarlet yelled, fighting her off. "You're the thief, aren't you? Admit it!"

By this point I had grabbed hold of Violet and managed to tug her back. She stood there in the dancing light, panting for breath as tears streamed down her cheeks. Emotions seemed to parade across her face; anger, despair, confusion, fear.

"I took those things for a reason!" yelled Violet. "She needed them!"

We all looked at the girl.

"Oh, skip it," Scarlet snapped. "Stop playing the victim, Violet. You're the one who's a thief. *And* a kidnapper!"

"I didn't kidnap her!" Violet shouted back. "I *rescued* her. Now are you going to listen, or what?"

"Shh," I said, dragging Scarlet back to us, grumbling all the way. "You're going to have the whole school running down here if you keep yelling!"

When we were all silent and Violet had recovered her composure, she began to speak. "Her name is Rose. I met her in... the asylum. Nobody understood her. They said she couldn't talk, that she was crazy. But she talks to me, don't you, Rose?"

"Yes, Miss Violet," said Rose, and her voice was soft and sweet.

"They called her 'princess' because of what she wrote down for the doctor... She said that her family was rich, that she was an heiress to a fortune. They all *laughed* at her. You should have heard them." Violet started pacing, and her fists were clenched with anger. "But it's all true. She swore it to me. Her family didn't want her. They wanted to get rid of her because of her problems... They had no other children and they thought her cousin would make a suitable heir if they could get her out of the way."

Rose was looking blank-faced at the wall throughout this speech, and if there was any flicker of recognition, I didn't see it. Was Violet telling the truth?

"So they locked her up in there and forgot about her, pretended she never existed and never came to visit her. But she was –" *sniff* – "she was the only person I could talk to. I knew I had to get her out of there, to rescue her from her cruel fate. And not let her parents steal her rightful fortune!"

"Or," said Scarlet, standing up again, "she's crazy and

dreamt this whole thing up, and you just went along with it because you heard the word 'fortune'! Or maybe you're just lying through your teeth! Where's your proof of any of this? I was locked up in the asylum too and I never saw either of you *once*."

"It's not like that," Violet snapped, nostrils flaring.

Suddenly, Rose moved towards her and tapped her on the arm. "Miss Violet," she said, "I think you're kind. And I don't think you tell lies."

"Rose and I were kept away from most of the patients," said Violet. "Especially you, Scarlet – they didn't want us to recognise each other and unpick what had happened. Did the doctors call you by the wrong name and tell you *all the time* that you were mad?"

Scarlet nodded, slowly.

"Me too. But I knew what Miss Fox did to me on that roof. I was determined not to disappear forever."

My twin stayed silent, taking all of this in. Could it be true?

I stared at the ghost girl, with her strange and delicate pale features. I noticed there was a golden locket around her neck – it certainly looked expensive. There was at least a chance that the story wasn't made up, and if it wasn't then she could be in danger. I knew that Scarlet hadn't deserved to be put in the asylum, and neither (unfortunately) had Violet.

Perhaps the same really was true for Rose.

"Please," said Violet, and it was in a tone of voice that I hadn't heard her use before – although to be fair, she hadn't said much at all since I'd been in her vicinity – one of desperation. "Please don't tell anyone about this."

"Because you'll get in trouble?" asked Scarlet.

"No! Because of what could happen to Rose. I need you all to swear that you won't tell anyone."

Rose clung to her arm, smiling vacantly. "The walls have been talking," she said.

"I'm not swearing anything until you explain yourself," Scarlet retorted. "How exactly did you escape?"

Violet pressed her trembling lips together, and shook her head. Before Scarlet could demand an answer, Ariadne piped up with a sudden realisation.

"So this is the reason you've been stealing," she said. "You've taken it all for Rose. The clothes, the food, the books…"

Violet sniffed. "I *had* to, don't you see? Please, swear you won't tell?"

We all looked at each other. There was anger in my twin's face and fear in my friend's. But I think we knew that, at least for the moment, we had to keep quiet about this. We needed enough time to decide what we were going to do.

"We swear," we said in unison, and with varying degrees

of enthusiasm.

There were a few moments of silence. That was, until I heard a creaking noise.

"What was that?" Ariadne whispered, her face filled with fright.

Another creak.

And another.

There was someone coming down the stairs.

They were moving slowly, as if it were difficult for them to walk. *Was it Mr Bartholomew?* I grabbed Scarlet's arm, my breathing quickening. She was staring at the dark doorway, her eyes wide.

Someone was coming, and there was nowhere for us to run.

It felt like an age. Each step was another closer to our fate. If it was the headmaster... would we even make it out alive?

But then a face appeared in the doorway, and it was not a face that any of us had been expecting.

"Miss Finch!" exclaimed Scarlet.

Our ballet teacher was staring back at us, clearly stunned. "Oh," was all she said.

"I can explain," my twin quickly started, just as Miss Finch blurted out the exact same thing.

Rose looked up. "Hello, Miss" she said in her tiny voice.

When Scarlet gets confused, she gets angry. "Right," she

said. "What *exactly* is going on here?"

Miss Finch sighed and leant against the door frame. "I presume you've found out about Rose, then?" She sounded incredibly weary.

Scarlet made a gesture that broadly said, *yes, that is quite apparent.*

"I got them both out," said Miss Finch, indicating Violet and Rose. "Since Scarlet was there under a false name, I thought it was possible that Violet was in there somewhere, too. I supposed Miss— my mother had inside knowledge from her time there. And my hunch was right – Violet was being kept there too." She took a deep breath. "I proved that Violet wasn't supposed to be there, and she was allowed to leave with me. But when she told me that Rose had been wrongfully imprisoned as well…"

Violet nodded, holding her chin high. Rose was still tugging on her sleeve.

"I shouldn't have done it, I know, and I'm afraid Rose is now rather on the run. Violet sneaked her out of the back entrance, by the fountain. I knew the guard, so I was able to distract him while they—"

"So you *were* both in the same place," I said, looking from Scarlet to Violet.

The ghost girl seemed to have stopped listening, but it was hard to tell with her. She was staring at the writing-covered wall.

Miss Finch nodded. "My mother had some influence there, it seems. She said they needed to be kept apart. After we rescued Scarlet, they moved the two girls back into the main ward."

There was a pause, and then I could have sworn I heard Rose mumble, "It's better here."

Better here? What a nightmare that asylum must have been, if a gloomy room deep under Rookwood School was preferable.

"So why is Rose down here in the cold, Miss?" asked Ariadne. Her face was drawn with worry.

"We needed to keep her safe until I could find somewhere better for her. I was afraid that the asylum would come looking. Or that I would be fired if she was discovered. She's vulnerable."

"You were going to tell me," Scarlet butted in, "the other day in the ballet studio. Weren't you? I knew there was something you were holding back, Miss."

"I decided you had enough to cope with in here," Miss Finch said gently. "I just wanted to make up for what my mother had done. Somehow."

I wondered about her, sometimes. In some ways she seemed as much an adult as any of the teachers, in others she seemed as lost as the rest of us.

She shook herself, then. "Girls, you shouldn't be down here." Scarlet raised a finger, clearly about to argue, but Miss Finch silenced her. "I know, I know I shouldn't, either. But it might not be safe, in more ways than one. You need to stay out of trouble."

"We will, Miss," I promised. Or at least, I hoped so.

"But..." she started, looking uncertain. "I can't keep coming down here night after night. Mr Bartholomew watches me like a hawk – he must think I'm plotting my mother's return, when nothing could be further from the truth!"

"We can help!" said Scarlet, eagerly. "We can take it in turns to bring Rose food and clothes. He won't be able to keep an eye on *all* of us, all the time."

"Miss Violet," Rose said, tugging on Violet's sleeve again, "the walls have been talking. Shouldn't we listen to them?"

"What do you mean?" asked Violet, exasperated.

Rose walked to the other side of the room as if she were in a dream, nearly knocking over one of the candles in the process.

"Careful," Violet warned, "you know you need to be careful with those!"

Rose stood in front of the far wall, staring up at it. The writing spread out across it like spiderwebs.

"Well, that's new," said Miss Finch, her eyes wide.

We all followed the ghost girl. "Rose," Violet whispered, "what have you done..."

Rose shook her head. "Not me." She pointed at the tapestry that lay in a pile on the cold floor. "It fell, and then the words came."

I looked at Scarlet, and I felt a shiver run down my spine.

If Rose hadn't written the words... then who had?

Chapter Fifteen

SCARLET

For a long time, I'd suspected I was insane. Now I was beginning to believe that everyone else was.

Ivy believed in ghosts, Violet and Miss Finch were hiding a girl in a secret room, and lord only knew what Ariadne was doing – she appeared to have pulled out a magnifying glass from *somewhere* and was peering at words that had appeared all over the stones. "It's paint," she was muttering. "Old, flaking paint..."

And as for the ghost girl herself, well... she was standing with her ear to the wall, as if it were talking to her.

I stepped closer, and I saw:

We are the Whispers in the Walls.
They will try to silence us, but they will fail.
We will speak out.
The truth MUST be revealed.
The truth about Rookwood. The truth about Headmaster
Bartholomew.
THE WHISPERS WILL BE HEARD.

I read it in amazement. What did this all mean? Who had written it? And when?

Below that, in smaller letters, there was yet more writing:

We pledge to:
  – Meet in one of the secret rooms once a week
  – Never tell anyone about the Whispers
  – Look, listen, learn everything we can
  – Collect evidence of the truth, searching high and low
  – Protect others
  – Uncover every detail of what REALLY goes on at
    this school!

And all around it were painted names, students' names, scattered around the text like fireflies.

Alice Jefferson. Elizabeth Fitzgerald. Ida Smith. Katy Morwen. Talia Yahalom. Bronwyn Jones. Emmeline Adel.

I felt shivers go down my spine.

I read that last name again.

And again.

"Ivy," I said. "Ivy, you need to look at this."

My sister came over to where I was standing, and her eyes followed mine.

"What..." Her hand came up to cover her mouth, and I saw her rereading it just as I had, in case her mind was playing a trick on her.

"It really says that, doesn't it?"

She nodded.

Emmeline Adel. *Our mother.*

Adel had been her maiden name, I remembered Father telling us that in some distant memory, foggy around the edges. It certainly wasn't a common name, that I was sure of. I supposed there was a chance that someone else could be called that, but it seemed unlikely.

Our mother? At Rookwood? We'd not known anything about it. We'd known very little about her, in fact. And now it seemed she'd not only been at the school, but been involved in this secret club, whatever it was.

"We need to get out of here," said Violet, suddenly edgy. "We should cover that back up, whatever it is. Rose needs to sleep, and I'm not about to let you lot get us caught..."

She had a point, but I was still angry with her. I thought that I'd get out of trouble by revealing her as the thief, not get into it up to my neck. What did all this *mean*?

"Shut up, Violet," I said. I turned to Ivy and Ariadne. "Will you remember this?" I gestured at the wall. "Until we can come back and copy it down? Make some sense of it?"

They nodded, though my twin still looked shocked.

"It's fascinating," said Ariadne. "A real mystery..."

"Then let's get out of here," I said. "I don't need this night getting any more bizarre." I looked Violet straight in the eye. "We'll keep your secret, but we're doing this for her," I pointed at Rose, "not you, all right?"

Miss Finch was still staring at the wall of words, the candlelight dancing across her eyes. "This is very interesting indeed," she said quietly.

"Miss?" I said. She looked back at me. "You should've told us about this. But... thank you, anyway. Thank you for getting us out of there."

Miss Finch smiled. "I just hope I haven't got you into even more trouble." Her eyes wandered back to the wall again. "All at Rookwood is not as it seems..."

I picked up one of the flickering candles and headed out

of the room, Ariadne and Ivy trailing behind me. My legs were heavy and I began to realise quite how tired I was. But my mind raced with everything we'd learnt.

Somehow, we made it back to room thirteen. Words were tumbling through my mind and threatening to spill out of my mouth, but they would have to wait until morning. I fell into bed, and as soon as I hit the sheets, I was asleep.

I woke up to a bright, frosty day, and for a moment everything seemed peaceful.

And then the morning bell drilled into my ears.

I sat up, clutching my head. "Ugh," I said.

To my surprise, Ivy was already sitting on the edge of her bed, looking over at me.

"Did all of that really happen?" I asked. "Or did I just have a particularly strange dream?"

"If you mean Violet and Miss Finch and the ghost girl and the secret room..." Ivy said. She didn't need to go on.

I dragged myself up and over to the mirror. Now *I* was the one who looked like a ghost. I was too pale and my hair was dishevelled. Instinctively, I reached for Mother's hairbrush – but my hand stopped just above it.

Those letters I'd seen every day of my life – E.G. – suddenly had new meaning.

"She was here," I muttered. I sat down on the stool in

front of the dressing table and swung round to face my twin. "Our mother was here. Can you believe it?"

"I suppose we can't say for sure that it wasn't someone with the same name," said Ivy. "But it seems very unlikely. Why didn't Father *say*?"

I shrugged, not wanting to think about Father. He never told us anything, why would he start now? "I wonder what she was like," I said, thinking aloud. "I mean... what house was she in? How did she wear her hair? Did she do ballet?"

I finally picked up the brush and dragged it through my hair, trying to tease out the tangles. Although my reflection in the mirror looked just like Ivy, I tried to imagine our mother there, but I couldn't do it. I only knew what she looked like from the one photograph that our stepmother hadn't thrown away.

"We know one thing about her," said Ivy, standing up. "She was in this secret society. *The Whispers in the Walls*. What do you think they were up to?"

I shivered a little at the mention of the name. It was uncomfortably close to my own nightmares. "Whoever they were, it sounds like they knew there were some dark dealings going on here. Maybe like what happened to me..."

"Well, we don't know exactly when it was written, Miss Fox may not have worked here then. But Mr Bartholomew definitely was, their message said so. But what could he have been doing?"

We both went silent then, our minds awash with horror as we thought of the strange man hunched over in his dark office. *I knew* there was something off about him.

"He can't..." Ivy started. "He can't be worse than Miss Fox... can he?"

Chapter Sixteen

Ivy

We stayed true to our word and kept quiet about Rose, and what's more, Ariadne managed to come to an agreement with Violet.

"We'll sneak bits of our food, biscuits and things, or whatever we've cooked in home ec," she said. "And we can buy more in the village shop on Saturday. That way Violet won't have to steal from the kitchens, and it won't be so suspicious."

I agreed, and Scarlet did too, though begrudgingly. She still thought that Violet and Miss Finch were crazy for trying to pull this off in the first place. I didn't really blame her – it wasn't exactly the most sensible of ideas.

But food wasn't the only problem. It was getting colder every day, and there was no heating or fireplace down in the secret room. Every time I glanced over at Violet during lessons, she looked preoccupied, worrying about Rose.

I couldn't help but wonder, though – was she really concerned for Rose because they were friends? Or because Violet saw it as an investment, if Rose's story about her family's huge fortune was true. Was she still Vile Violet, the same person who had tormented and stolen from Scarlet, who had been nothing but selfish? Or had she truly changed for the better? Hearing that she'd been locked in the asylum too brought all the misery of visiting the place flooding back. And mixed in with this was a curious feeling – one I'd never thought I'd have regarding Violet – sympathy.

"I can't stop thinking about it," Ariadne said one lunchtime. "The Whispers, I mean. Just imagine, your own mother..."

I took a sip of my tea. "I know. I just wish there was a way to find out more about it."

Before that week, all I'd known about my mother was that her name was Emmeline, that she'd once owned a string of pearls and a hairbrush, and that she'd been married to our father. I had a vague idea of what she'd looked like. Suddenly

I had to add to that list that she'd attended Rookwood School and been involved in some sort of conspiracy to expose the headmaster, and I really wasn't sure what to do with that information.

"Maybe there is a way," said Ariadne, and her eyes had that unfocused look that told me she had seen something I hadn't. "Do you remember what the first one of their pledges was?"

I shook my head. "Something about meeting in the secret room?"

She waved a sugar lump at me. "Meeting in the secret *rooms*. It was plural!"

"Oh lord," said Scarlet, sitting down with her tray. "Is she having ideas again?"

"Secret rooms!" said Ariadne, waving her hands about and nearly hurling the sugar at Josephine Wilcox. I took it off her before she could do any damage.

Scarlet raised an eyebrow, intrigued. "There's more than one?"

"It would seem so," I said, and quickly I was the one whose mind was somewhere else. *If we found another room, would we find out more about the Whispers? Would we find out more about our mother?*

"We could look, I suppose," my twin mused, "but we don't have the first clue where to start."

"Hmm. I'll think about it," said Ariadne. She picked up another sugar lump and ate it with a crunch.

As Scarlet and I walked to get changed for ballet, we ran into Penny. That was never pleasant at the best of times, but she appeared to be particularly angry. She was leaning against the door of the geography classroom, her arms folded and a frown plastered across her freckled face.

"What are you doing?" Scarlet asked.

"I was *supposed* to be meeting Violet," she sneered. Then she started muttering under her breath: "The first time she speaks to me in months and she doesn't even turn up... I want to find out exactly where she is meant to have been 'abroad' – an 'exclusive French academy', wasn't it? As if she'd just leave me like that! There's something going on and I intend to find out what!"

I was all in favour of carrying on past, but Scarlet couldn't leave it alone. "I thought best friends told each other everything," she said in mock pity.

Penny's frown deepened. "I thought so too," she said, and for a moment there was sadness in her voice. Then she looked straight at Scarlet and her usual self returned. "But it's none of your business!"

I grabbed hold of Scarlet's arm, worried we were going to be late. I hated disappointing Miss Finch. My twin didn't resist this time, and we turned to leave.

"Unless..." said Penny.

We stopped.

She darted in front of us. "Unless you know what's going on. Has she told you anything?"

"No," I said, at the same time as Scarlet said, "What are you talking about?"

"She's hiding something. And you two are just as suspicious as she is. The *old* Violet would never have stood me up!"

"Violet hates me, and the feeling is mutual," said Scarlet. "What makes you think I would care what she's getting up to?"

Penny changed tack and pulled out her red prefect book. "If you don't know anything about Violet, maybe you know something about the thefts? Maybe you want to confess? I'm sure I'll find *some* evidence against you..."

Scarlet snorted. "Write my name down in your book as many times as you like, Winchester, it's not going to change anything." She barged past, dragging me with her.

"I'll get you for this, Scarlet! I'll get you back for everything! You'll regret framing me for breaking that stupid piano!" Penny shouted, but we carried on down the corridor. She sounded like a toddler having a tantrum, and I knew Scarlet would dismiss everything she'd said. But Penny was a force to be reckoned with, that much I knew.

We were just in time for ballet, hurrying down the stone stairs in our leotards. It was freezing as usual in the studio, and I began to worry about Rose again. And wasn't she lonely, down there in the dark?

Miss Finch greeted us cheerily, with only the faintest flicker of a wink to me and Scarlet. "Let's get moving, girls. There's a reason it's called a warm-up…"

She sat at her piano and I was glad to see such a familiar sight after all the weirdness of the week. I began to let loose as I practised at the *barre*, my body easily sliding into the positions that I knew so well.

Penny ran in, late.

Miss Finch looked up. "Where have you been, Penny?" she asked.

"I was…" she panted. "I'm…"

Our instructor waited for an excuse, but none came. She sighed and stood up, pushing on the piano lid for support, and walked over to Penny.

I looked at Scarlet, and then back at the mirror. We all pretended that we weren't listening.

"You wanted to come back to this class, didn't you?" Miss Finch asked gently.

"Yes, Miss."

"Then, please, do take it seriously. Don't give me a reason to have you removed again. Unless you'd prefer another sport? Lacrosse? Swimming?"

My skin crawled as I remembered my ill-fated swimming lesson. I was pretty sure that Penny wouldn't fancy that, either.

"No, Miss," she replied. "S-sorry, Miss."

"All right," said Miss Finch. She walked over to the wall of mirrors and began going down the class and checking our positions, while Penny hastily laced on her shoes. She saw me looking at her and glared.

Hmmph. I turned back to my reflection. It was considerably more friendly.

I lay in bed that night, thankful that the small metal radiator in the corner of room thirteen had finally come to life. It didn't give out much heat, but it was enough to make the temperature more bearable.

For the first time in ages, I was awake while Scarlet wasn't. She'd slipped off to sleep not long after lights out, leaving me alone in the dark.

There was a knocking on our door.

It was soft at first, and I wasn't sure if I was imagining it. I tucked the covers over my head and tried to shut it out.

But it got louder, and then I was certain that it *was*

knocking. "*Scarlet*," I hissed. "Wake up!"

And as I sat up in bed, the door flung open.

It was Violet.

"Rose is gone!"

Chapter Seventeen

SCARLET

Ivy shook me awake. "What?" I asked groggily. "What's going on?" For once I had managed to fall into a deep, dreamless sleep and now someone was trying to drag me out of it.

"Rose is missing," she said.

I opened my eyes and saw my twin's worried face in the moonlight. Even more worrying was the sight of Violet, who was standing just inside the doorway.

"I've searched the whole library and most of the building," Violet said, her voice just loud enough to be heard but not so loud as to arouse suspicion. "I must have forgotten to bolt the door. She's nowhere to be found! You have to help me look for her!"

"Why?"

Violet gasped, clearly affronted. *Of course* she'd just decided that we had to help her.

"It's not our problem, is it?" I said. "You're the one who decided to keep her as a pet. Why should we risk getting kicked out of school just to help *you*?"

"It's not for me," she insisted. "It's Rose. Anything could have happened to her!"

I looked over at Ivy, who had perched nervously on the edge of her bed, and I could already tell that she'd made up her mind. "Come on, Scarlet," she said. "She really could be in danger."

Ugh. I peeled off my covers and went to pull on my coat and shoes. I pointed at Violet. "I'm not doing this for you," I said.

"Where's Ariadne?" Ivy asked.

"Couldn't wake her," whispered Violet, as we sneaked out of the room. "She just muttered something about not wanting any flowers and went back to sleep."

Ivy and I followed Violet along the corridor and down the stairs. I couldn't believe what was happening in a way – my hatred of Violet hadn't diminished at all, and I felt nauseous even being reminded of her and of how she had made my life hell. Now I was letting her lead me around like a puppet. I would've given up and turned back, had it not been for Ivy. I didn't want her falling out with me again, not after I'd only just persuaded her to trust me.

"Where are we even going?" I asked quietly, as we reached the bottom.

"Outside," said Violet. "I mean, I've looked everywhere else. Everywhere that's not locked, that is."

Great. Just great. "But it's freezing out. Are you crazy? They should've left you in the asylum."

She spun round to face me. "Don't you *ever* say that again!"

I shrugged. I knew what it was like, I was allowed to say it. "Let's just find her, all right?"

In silence we found the nearest door that led outside. It was usually locked with a bolt, but it had been slid back. Maybe Rose *had* gone outside. Violet tugged it open and we stepped outside, the cold air hitting us like a brick wall.

"We should... split up," Ivy suggested, suddenly breathless. "And we can meet back here if we can't find her."

I agreed. The further away I could get from Violet, the better.

So Ivy headed towards the stables, I made for the swimming pool and Violet started walking in the direction of the playing fields. I really hoped that Rose wanted to be found, because I didn't have much hope for any of us spotting her if she didn't. The moon was bright but it slid in and out of the clouds, and the faint stars didn't shine enough to light our way.

As my eyes adjusted to the gloom, I felt my way around the wall of the changing rooms. I tried the door – locked.

I turned to the pool and stared into the dark water. There was nothing, no movement. I remembered the girl who had drowned, and suddenly felt ill. Was this where it had happened?

There was a cry from the direction of the stables.

I ran back over the gravel, the sudden burst of movement warming my bones. My heart raced. *Ivy?*

Skidding around the corner, I came into the stable yard. Ivy was standing by one of the stalls, her hand over her mouth.

"Sorry," she said quietly, as I approached. "She startled me." She pointed into the stall.

I peered in over the door, and I could just make out the flash of Rose's eyes in the darkness. She was curled up in the straw beside a snoozing pony, looking perfectly at home. "Rose, what are you—" I started, before remembering that she wouldn't talk to us. I shook my head and leant against the wall to get my breath back.

A moment later, Violet came running. "I thought I heard something," she said, panic in her voice. "Have you found her?"

I waved at the stable. "She fancied a night-time pony ride, apparently."

Violet ignored me and poked her head in the stall door. The pony lifted its head and whinnied at her. "Rose," she said, "why are you out here? You know I told you to stay in the room."

"I wanted to go outside," I heard Rose say quietly. "I didn't know it was night-time. And it is so cold. But the ponies are warm."

I was annoyed, but I felt a pang of sympathy. It really was freezing – all the hairs on my arms were standing up, and I couldn't wait to get back to room thirteen and my bed. Rose didn't even have a proper bed of her own, or any heating.

"You need to sort this out, Violet," I said. "Make sure she knows she has to stay inside. And get her more blankets, or something. Otherwise she's going to keep running away."

"I thought you didn't care?" Violet snapped back. "Anyway, I will. Come on out now, Rose. It's okay..."

Rose came to the door and stepped out. Her dress was covered in straw and she smelt slightly of horse, but she seemed fine. "I used to have a pony," she said to Violet, in her tiny voice. "They're wonderful, aren't they?"

I snorted. She would get on well with Ariadne. Ivy would have said she was a kind heart. Unlike some people I could think of.

As if to prove my point, Violet quickly led her away without a word of thanks. *Typical*.

"I bet she doesn't *really* care that much about this girl," I said to Ivy as soon as she was out of earshot. "She was probably just frightened that her new inheritance had gone out the window. Anyway, come on, let's get back inside. I'm dying of cold here!"

Chapter Eighteen

Ivy

I thought it couldn't get any colder than that night. I was wrong. It got so cold that we were shivering in the classrooms and blowing on our hands to keep them from seizing up while we were writing. In geography I could have sworn that there was ice in my inkwell.

We managed to find Rose a spare blanket to keep her warm, and keep her hidden for a while longer. Ariadne used her pocket money to pick up some food from Kendall and Smith's in the nearby village – stuff that would last as long as possible, like tinned fruit and cornflakes. I hoped Miss Finch would soon think of a safer location for Rose. We trusted our ballet teacher, but I wondered how long the situation could last – and how long it would be before we got caught.

As I yawned through a dull assembly the following week, I was surprised to see Mr Bartholomew taking the stage.

He looked even worse than before, if that was possible. He was almost bent double at the podium, and his face was pale as milk.

For a moment I panicked. It was rare for him to make an appearance at assembly. What if someone had found out about Rose? What if they knew we were involved? I gripped the edges of my seat a little tighter.

"Good morning, girls." The headmaster's voice rattled across the hall. "I have been informed that there have been... no further thefts. This is good to hear. Rest assured that the culprit will still be severely punished if they are discovered. But it seems... we will not have to cancel our traditional event, after all."

There was a buzz of puzzled murmuring from the first years. I quickly glanced at Ariadne, who looked equally confused, and Scarlet, who suddenly looked rather horrified.

"For those of you who do not know," he droned on, "we have an annual morning of ice skating, when the lake freezes over, as a... mmhmm, special treat. The lake has been inspected and is... solid enough to skate on."

He broke out into a fit of coughing, and grabbed the podium, looking for a moment as though he was going to fall off the stage.

Mrs Knight rushed over, her face worried.

The headmaster stopped coughing and looked up at her – even from a distance away, I could tell that his eyes were bloodshot. "Ah yes," he said. "Mrs Knight will fill you in, I'm sure." He skulked away and out of the door at the side of the hall.

I breathed a sigh of relief. He made me edgy, and knowing that all those years ago my own mother had tried to expose him for his activities made it even worse. What was he getting away with?

Mrs Knight watched him go. "Ahem," she said. "Yes. In a moment I'll ask all the first and second years to file out. Go to your dorms and put your warmest clothes on. You'll select a pair of skates, and then we will all walk down to the lake. Stay in pairs, please."

Instinctively, I took Scarlet's hand. Ariadne's face dropped. "Oh, sorry..." I whispered.

"It's all right," she sighed. "I'll find someone." As if by magic, Dot Campbell waved at her from a few rows away, and her expression brightened.

Despite that, I still felt guilty. Scarlet smirked at Ariadne, but I gave her a slap and she soon stopped. Could it be that my always-confident sister was actually jealous of my friendship with Ariadne? Curious...

"The rest of you will have the opportunity to go on other days," Mrs Knight continued, "assuming that the weather continues in this manner." She looked out of one of the tall windows that lined the hall. "And it seems that will be the case."

Outside, the first flakes of snow were falling.

We headed back to the room. "Ice skating's horrible," said Scarlet. "It's awful."

"It can't be that bad—" I started.

"It *is* that bad. If you don't die of cold then the blades will get you! I can't believe they think it's a *treat*! Can't we just hide?"

My twin had a penchant for exaggerating, and I felt sure that she was making it out to be a lot worse than it really was. We had been ice skating a few times when we were younger, and I'd always enjoyed it. Once you got your balance, you could zip around quickly, the wind whipping your hair. It was like ballet, in a way.

"I'm sure it'll be fine," I said.

Scarlet looked completely unconvinced.

"What are you, a coward?" I teased.

That worked. She marched on ahead of me purposefully, and when I got back to room thirteen she'd already started getting changed.

I pulled on my cardigan and coat. Scarlet buttoned on two extra cardigans and somehow found a woolly hat as well. I wasn't sure it would be *that* cold, but then it wasn't exactly warm and toasty in our room. I found myself wishing that I'd brought some gloves at least.

We joined the queue of girls snaking around the swimming pool changing rooms. The snow fell lightly on our heads, speckling our coats with flecks of white. I shivered as we waited, slowly shuffling forward. I spotted Ariadne join the line behind us with Dot in tow, and felt a pang of guilt again. At least they looked happy.

I couldn't say the same for Scarlet. Her face was miserable.

Regardless of what my twin said, I was looking forward to ice skating. It couldn't be *that* bad.

We finally made it to the door of the changing rooms, where Miss Bowler was waiting. She handed me a pair of skates. "Put those on," she said.

Ah.

The skates looked, well, hideous. They were a dirty brown with fraying laces. They looked like they'd been shoved on to girls' feet for the past fifty years and never been given a clean. I was fairly sure they were several sizes too small, and the blades were both sharp and rusted.

I shuddered, and this time the cold wasn't responsible.

"Well?" Miss Bowler barked. "Get on with it!" I realised I'd been standing there staring at the horrible things and not moving. I heard Scarlet snickering behind me.

Sighing, I headed back outside. A moment later, Scarlet came over – her amusement had been short-lived, because she'd been given a pair that were *enormous*.

"Do they not try and –" I waved vaguely at the skates – "find ones that actually fit people?"

"That would take too long," said my twin, rolling her eyes.

We followed the other girls back around the side of the school and out across the grounds in the direction of the lake.

I'd never been down to the lake before, only seen it from a distance or from up on the rooftop. The path to it led down through a thick copse of trees that blocked out the grey sky, and eventually opened out on to a barren shore. Some of the trees hung their branches down almost as far as the surface, as if they were trying to stroke it with long bony fingers.

The lake spread out in front of us, as grey as the sky above. A few of the girls had already braved the ice, and the shiny surface was criss-crossed with thin lines. Some clearly knew what they were doing and darted around, pulling off twirls and fast turns, while others were giggling as they clung desperately to their friends.

I turned to Scarlet. "It looks fun," I said. "Despite these monstrosities." I took a seat on a fallen log and tried to pull the skates on. It took several attempts to force my feet into them. I caught my finger on the sharp blade. *Ouch.* I sucked at it, leaving a spot of iron-tasting blood on my thumb.

Scarlet was standing there with her arms folded, looking haughty. "They can't make me do it."

"Oh yes, we can," said Miss Bowler, suddenly appearing behind her. She gave Scarlet a rough pat on the back, really more of a slap. "Get your skates on!" she bellowed. "Builds character!"

My twin sat down beside me and muttered furiously as she tugged on her own lethal skates.

I managed to stand up and tottered over the frozen ground to the ice. *One step...* Then I pushed off with one foot and I was gliding, slipping across the top of the lake. I wobbled and threw my arms out to steady myself. *How do you stop?* I thought as I came perilously close to another girl. It took me a moment, but I remembered: knees in, slight turn, shift your weight. My skate shaved up a little pile of snow as I skidded to a halt, breathless.

"Ivy!" someone shouted.

I looked around. It was Ariadne, waving to me from the edge. I watched as she took two steps onto the ice and immediately fell on her bottom.

Mrs Knight stepped forward and offered her a hand, but Miss Bowler was simply yelling: "Up, up! Falling is for quitters!"

Poor Ariadne...

Scarlet skated up behind me uncertainly. She grabbed my arm and her momentum almost pulled me over, but I started moving too, until we were skating in synch.

"You can hold me up," Scarlet laughed, seeming a little more enthusiastic.

We weaved in and out of the other girls, trying to keep in step as we circled the lake. The cold air that whipped at our faces was at least a refreshing change to being trapped indoors. Though my feet ached and I was sure I would have blisters before long, I was beginning to enjoy myself.

And that was when things began to go *very* wrong.

As we crossed over to one side of the lake, past a rocky outcrop just out of sight of the teachers, I heard shouting.

"...ignoring me, like I mean nothing to you!"

"Do you have *any idea* what I went through? Why didn't you come looking for me?"

Scarlet and I skidded to a halt. A small crowd was forming against the rocks. I peered around, wondering whose argument we had just skated into.

It was Penny and Violet.

"How could I? I was stuck here." That was Penny, and there was fierce anger painted all over her face. I supposed she had just found out about the asylum.

I could only see Violet from the back. "The *twins* managed to find each other, didn't they? I bet it wasn't that hard." I frowned. Her voice was dripping with derision.

"Shut up!" Penny screamed. "I know there's more to this! What have you been playing at since you got back?"

"I don't know what you're talking about." Violet's arms were folded, and she seemed oblivious to us watching.

"You're lying! I always *know* when you're lying!"

"I don't lie, you evil *witch*!"

With a roar of frustration, Penny shoved Violet as hard as she could.

I watched as time seemed to slow down. Violet lost her balance. She toppled, arms raised out to the sky. There was a sickening crack. Then there was a splash.

Violet had fallen through the ice.

Chapter Nineteen

SCARLET

Violet disappeared under the dark water. Someone started screaming.

And then she reappeared, thrashing and waving her arms.

"Help her!" Ethel cried out.

Penny didn't move, frozen like the ice beneath her feet. Didn't even say a word.

I looked around. No one was doing anything, just staring in horror. It was Violet. Violet who I *hated* more than anything. But I couldn't stand by and let her drown.

Could I?

"Go and get one of the teachers," I yelled to Ivy, knowing that she was quick on her feet. She nodded at me, breathless and horrified, and skated away.

How could I get near Violet? There was a danger that if I skated towards her I'd fall straight into the gaping hole, and besides, there were already treacherous-looking cracks spreading out around it.

Thinking quickly, I crouched down until I was I on my hands and knees. The cold stung my skin where I touched the slippery surface, but I kept crawling forward. Violet's cries and choking echoed in my ears.

"Stop panicking, Violet!" I shouted. "Just keep your head above the water! Ivy's getting someone!"

Someone was still screaming – Nadia, I realised. I wished she'd shut up. Violet needed to stay calm if we were going to get her out of there.

Soon I was near enough to her, but I didn't dare go any closer in case I fell in myself. "Get to the edge and see if you can hold on to it," I said. She looked up at me, terror in her wide eyes as she kicked her legs and felt for the surface. She managed to raise her arms, her breathing still frantic.

"Help," she managed to choke out.

She was within arm's reach, just. I gripped her frozen hand. "Stay calm," I ordered. "Help's on the way."

Thankfully I was right, because I wasn't sure if I could stay there much longer. Miss Bowler came running along the shore, carrying a life ring on one arm.

"Get off the ice! All of you!" she panted.

Nadia's screams had dissolved into sobs, but she quickly skated to safety, taking her minions with her.

Only Penny didn't move. She was still standing there, looking down at what she'd done. I honestly couldn't tell if she was horrified or proud.

"I said ALL OF YOU, Miss Winchester! MOVE!"

Penny turned and hobbled ashore.

I looked up at Miss Bowler, pleadingly. I didn't think I could physically let go of Violet's hand. She was clinging so tight I thought that my own would drop off.

"Help me!" she cried.

"Scarlet, get this to her!" Miss Bowler said. She tossed me the life ring.

Violet instinctively grabbed it, but it was clear she didn't want to let go of my hand. "Just let go!" I said. "You need to take the ring with both hands!" She slowly and painfully unclenched her fist and took hold.

"Get back, Scarlet," Miss Bowler called out.

I turned on my hands and knees. I heard a *crack* as another sliver of ice snapped under me. *Oh no.*

I was facing the shore now, and I looked up and saw Ivy

standing there. There was a look of pure horror on her face.

She thinks she might lose me again, I realised.

The thought was enough to spur me on. I crawled faster and faster, ignoring the cold and the fracturing of the surface below me. I built up momentum and slid the final few feet, rolling over and over on to the hard stones of the shore.

I sat up, gasping for breath. Miss Bowler was pulling on the rope attached to the life ring with all her might. "Help me pull!" she ordered. A chain of girls grabbed the rope and heaved too. I kicked off my too-big skates and joined in, then Ivy was behind me.

And before we knew it, Violet was sliding out of the ice.

One of her skates had gone, sucked under by the current. The other scraped along as we pulled her towards us. Her limbs had gone limp – she lay there silently, eyes wide, and then the shivers spread over her. She started shaking violently on the ground, her hair and clothes soaking.

I watched as Ivy pulled off her coat and wrapped it around her. A few others did the same.

"We need to get her inside," said Miss Bowler.

We all helped Violet up and began the long, arduous trek back to the school.

Mrs Knight met us near the doors with the school nurse, armed with a hastily gathered pile of blankets.

"What happened?" asked Nurse Gladys.

"She fell through the ice," said Miss Bowler. "She needs to go inside, NOW."

The nurse evidently agreed. "Mrs Knight, we need to get her in some lukewarm water to get her temperature back to normal."

Mrs Knight nodded. Together, she and the nurse half-dragged Violet inside.

"Violet didn't fall," said Nadia. Ivy and I turned to look at her. "She was PUSHED."

Miss Bowler swung around. "Excuse me?"

"Penny pushed her!" Nadia shrieked. "She pushed her on to the ice!"

"I did *not*!" Penny yelled back. "I... I didn't mean to!"

And suddenly they'd jumped at each other. We stood back aghast as they scratched and pulled each other's hair, their screams blurring together.

It was over in seconds, as Miss Bowler grabbed them both by the scruff of the neck and held them at arm's length. "BOTH OF YOU. MR BARTHOLOMEW'S OFFICE. NOW!"

She dragged them away.

The rest of the day's lessons were cancelled as the teachers dealt with the 'incident'. I guessed ice skating was probably off the menu from now on.

I spent most of the afternoon wrapped in my blanket, huddled up against our small radiator. I still couldn't stop my teeth chattering.

Ivy and Ariadne sat on Ivy's bed. Ariadne kept recounting the tale of the terrible accident and our daring rescue, as if she'd somehow been involved and not been flat on her back at the other side of the lake. I rolled my eyes.

"Ice skating is horrible," she finished.

Ivy was staring at me.

"I told you so," I said.

"I don't understand," Ariadne said. "I thought Penny and Violet were friends."

"They're both vicious," I said. "You wouldn't want to cross either of them. And now they've crossed *each other*. This isn't going to end well."

Ivy bit her lip, and I knew she was thinking about what had happened to me.

I hadn't really spoken about it, but somehow the words came tumbling out. "They dragged me on to the roof, didn't they? What do you think Violet was going to do? What if she'd thrown me off? If Miss Fox hadn't taken her..." I stared at the wall. It was something I'd not even wanted to think about.

Ivy climbed off her bed and came and sat down beside me

on the floor. "That's not going to happen again," she said, firmly.

"No," I said, "but who knows what they'll do?" I snapped out of it, and turned to my twin. "Penny nearly *killed* Violet today."

"She..." Ariadne started. "I thought she'd changed. That night when we finally found out about everything that had happened with Miss Fox, she seemed to really care about finding you and Violet."

"Penny cares about *being in charge*," I said. "She cares about being popular and bossing everyone around like she owns the place. I don't know if she cares about *people*."

"Speaking of caring for people –" Ivy looked worried – "we're going to have to check on Rose more often. I don't know how she'll cope without Violet. I mean, they were always together in the asylum." Suddenly she went silent.

"What is it?" I asked, after a few long moments of silence.

"You know..." she said. "On the roof. When it all happened. We wondered how Miss Fox managed to take Violet away without you seeing."

"We found another hatch," Ariadne chimed in. "A trapdoor."

Hmm. That made sense, I supposed. It was one thing that had made me doubt myself.

Ivy nodded. "We know the Whispers had more than

one secret room, right? And they said something about 'searching high and low'. Maybe that was actually a clue? Maybe you have to search high... to find the trapdoor?"

I sat up, my attention caught. "You could be right. And if you are... *what's on the other side of that trapdoor?*"

Chapter Twenty

IVY

I couldn't believe I hadn't remembered it before. It seemed so obvious now that I thought about it. We *had* to get into that room to see if it contained any more clues about the Whispers.

"One problem," said Ariadne. "It was locked, wasn't it?"

I started to laugh.

"What?"

"When has that ever stopped us before?"

"Point taken."

"But," I realised, "we don't know where the keys are kept any more, now that Miss Fox is gone. I wouldn't even know where to start."

"Maybe the caretaker has copies of them," said Ariadne. "Or Mr Bartholomew."

I frowned. I couldn't think of anything I wanted to do less than attempt to break into the headmaster's office.

"We could break through the trapdoor," said Scarlet.

I looked at her. "Are you mad?"

"So I've been told. I'm serious, though. If it's wooden, you can smash through it."

I almost made a comment about smashing pianos, but I thought better of it. "Are you volunteering?"

Scarlet's face went paler and she burrowed into her blanket. "No," she said. "I'm not... I'm not going to go up there, all right?" Her breathing sounded shallow and panicked.

Of course. I should have thought before I spoke. "Sorry," I said, gently.

"I'll do it!" said Ariadne.

I put my head in my hands. "This is a terrible idea."

It *was* a terrible idea. But we also had the afternoon off. Everyone was staying inside to keep warm, and the teachers were distracted by the whole situation between Penny and

Violet. If ever there was a time to try out a terrible idea, this was it.

Scarlet had refused to go on the mission, and that was fine by me and Ariadne. There was no way I was forcing her to go back on the roof again. The idea clearly terrified her.

Ariadne and I wrapped up in our warmest clothes (I persuaded Scarlet to give me her hat) and we trekked up Rookwood's winding stairs to the top floor and the hatch that led out on to the roof. Thankfully, the last time it had been opened was by us, and apparently no one had checked the padlock since then. We unlatched it and climbed out into a world of swirling white.

The snow was falling a little more heavily now, but it still wasn't quite settling. It flurried around us. I pulled my coat up around my mouth. "Careful, Ariadne," I warned. "It's a long way down." She nodded back at me, determined.

Slowly but surely we made our way across the roof, climbing over the peaks and sliding down the other side, past the chimney stack, until we came to the other hatch.

It was right where I'd remembered it. The trapdoor was old, made of wood that looked a little rotten and woodworm-chewed. "It's really ragged," I said, raising my voice to be heard over the wind. "Maybe it will break."

"What can we hit it with, though?"

I looked around. The nearest available object was a stray

brick. I picked it up, blowing on my freezing hands to try and warm them, and slammed it down on to the trapdoor.

Nothing happened.

"Rats," I said.

"There's got to be a way," said Ariadne.

And before I could say anything, she had sprung on top of the hatch and was bouncing up and down.

"Maybe if we jump on it, it might loosen it a biiiiiiiit—"

"Ariadne?!" I yelled down. "Are you all right?"

There was silence. And then, "Ouch." And then, "Yes." And then, "I think I fell on a bed!"

A bed?

I crouched down and peered through the hole. I could just make out Ariadne sprawled on a mattress, surrounded by pieces of shattered wood that had once been a bed. She waved cheerfully at me.

"It's not far," she called up. "And the bed is quite springy. Jump down!"

I watched as she shuffled off the mattress. *Gulp.* It was now or never. After peeling away the remaining fragments of the trapdoor, I stood up, took a deep breath, and jumped.

Even with the mattress to cushion me, the fall still knocked the air out of my lungs. "Oof," was all I could say.

My eyes adjusted to the light and I took in the room around

me. It was on the small side, not much bigger than our own, and it was filled with... broken furniture. Wonky bed frames leant up against the wall, a smashed mirror, a chair with three legs, an enormous wardrobe with the door hanging ajar, and all of it covered with thick dust and cobwebs.

I noticed the ladder, fallen haphazardly against a lopsided chest of drawers. I pointed it out to Ariadne. "Look – that must be how Miss Fox got down here with Violet."

Ariadne nodded. "You know," she said thoughtfully, "just because it's full of rubbish, doesn't mean this *wasn't* one of the Whispers' secret rooms. If they had a key –" she gestured at the locked door – "or knew how to get in through the trapdoor, it would be a great meeting place. Not much chance of being caught by any teachers up here."

She was right. "We should search," I said. I stood up and tried to brush some of the dust off my dress, but I was still coated in it. "There could be something here."

Right. As Ariadne went over to some of the piles of wood and scrutinised them, I tried to think of a more logical way of doing this. If the Whispers had hidden anything in here that hadn't been found, it was probably *inside* something. There were only a few things in the room that could still hold anything, namely the drawers and the wardrobe.

I tried the drawers. Each one was empty, apart from one, which held a discarded sock that I threw away in disgust.

The wardrobe, then. I tugged on the side that was closed, but when it was open there was nothing visible inside. "Drat," I said aloud. "Nothing in here."

Ariadne came over to me. "Hang on, what's that?"

I looked where she was pointing. Just under the grime, there was a thin line in a rectangle running around the base of the wardrobe. *Oh my.* I had a feeling I knew what this was, and it was a trick that Scarlet had used before.

I reached in and dug my nails into the crack, and then I pulled up the wood.

"A false bottom!" Ariadne gasped.

And sure enough, there was something in there. A book.

My friend reached in and took hold of it. It was in good condition, having been hidden from the outside world for so long.

I recognised it immediately. The red cover, the golden rook and oak tree. "It's a prefect book!" But that wasn't all – someone had written:

The Whispers

in swirling ink.

Ariadne waved it at me. "At least one of them was a prefect! That's like being a double agent! How intriguing!"

"We don't know that yet. What does it say? Open it up!"

Trembling with excitement, Ariadne peeled back the first page.

And her face fell.

Chapter Twenty-One

SCARLET

I waited patiently in our room for Ivy and Ariadne to return. Well, maybe *impatiently* would be more accurate. I bit my nails and doodled in my diary and paced up and down wrapped in the blanket.

With five minutes to go before dinner, I was wondering if I should go and look for them. But the mere thought of going to the rooftop made me nauseous. It haunted my nightmares – sometimes I dreamt I was trapped in the walls, but other times I was back on the roof, right on the edge, the dizzying heights spread out before me, and Violet laughing as she pushed me off. I always woke up with a start before I hit the ground.

But I was worrying for nothing, because just then Ariadne burst through the door and shook what looked like a prefect book at me. "We found this!" she said. "But we don't know what it says!"

"What? Give that here..." I took it off her and stared at it as Ivy entered the room. "Eh? It's just numbers!"

Ivy looked dejected. "I think it's a code. The whole thing's written in it."

It certainly looked that way. Rows and rows of numbers, with dashes in between. I guessed that was how they'd managed to keep their secrets for all these years.

7-19-22
4-19-18-8-11-22-9-8
18-13
7-19-22
4-26-15-15-8

"But if it's a code, then we can break it, right?" I said.

Ariadne brightened at that. "True!"

"You get on it then, brainbox," I said, tossing the book back at her. "If it says anything about our mother, I want to know."

"I'll do it," she grinned.

We hid the Whispers' book in the old hole in my mattress and headed down for dinner. Ariadne stayed uncharacteristically quiet as we walked – she was puzzling out the code in her mind, probably. I wanted her to crack it, of course, but... could we trust her? She seemed like such a goody two-shoes, and I couldn't help but think she'd end up turning the book in to the teachers or something. Then we'd *really* be for it.

Dinner was, surprisingly, not stew. It was, apparently, a casserole.

Ivy took a bite of it. "Are they sure this isn't stew?" she said. "Because it tastes a lot like the stew."

I sighed. I was famished, and I still hadn't quite warmed up. It didn't taste brilliant, but it *was* hot, and that made all the difference.

There was no sign of Penny or Nadia. I wondered what Mr Bartholomew would do with them. What would their punishment be? I shuddered to think.

"I've got it," said Ariadne, snapping her fingers so loudly that everyone stared at her.

"Got what?" asked Mrs Knight from the other side of the table. She looked a little frazzled.

"Nothing," Ariadne mumbled. Her cheeks flushed red.

"Um, Ariadne was trying to solve a... difficult maths problem," Ivy said.

"Oh, well. Jolly good," said Mrs Knight. "I like to see a keen student."

As the rest of the table returned to chatting, Ariadne leant forward and whispered conspiratorially, "It wasn't a maths problem!"

"We know," I said.

"Oh." She paused. "I've figured out the code, I think! I'll just need a while to transcribe it all."

Hmm. "Keep it a secret, you swear?" I said.

Ariadne blinked at me. "Of course!"

I frowned. I'd have to make sure she stayed true to her word.

Penny and Nadia were back in class the following day, made to sit on opposite sides of the room and forbidden from going near each other. They both looked miserable and moved awkwardly, like they were in pain. Nadia's cheeks were streaked with tears. Even the thought of facing Mr Bartholomew's wrath made me wince.

Violet was still in the sick bay. We'd sent Ariadne down to see Rose in the night, to give her food and a mug of water and – *ick* – take her to the lavatories. I was expecting Ariadne to be a mouse about it, but she seemed to be worried enough about Rose to be willing to risk the consequences of being caught roaming the school at night.

I sat scratching my desk with my compasses, and realised that I was worrying about Rose as well. It was dark down there, and cold. What if she was afraid?

Shut up, I told myself. *Rose isn't your problem.*

Ivy's wet-blanketness – sorry, *sensitivity* – was rubbing off on me.

I wasn't looking forward to sharing ballet class with Penny. I wished someone would order her to stay away from *me*.

The ballet studio had never been warm, but now that the temperature had plummeted it was unbearable, like walking into an icebox.

Miss Finch was sitting at her piano wearing a scarf and a woolly hat. "Sorry about this, girls," she said, rubbing her hands together. "I'm afraid more dancing is our only option."

Ivy and I sat down and tried to lace on our shoes with stiff hands. And that was when Penny walked in and sat down beside me. I waited for her to say *something*, some sarcastic comment, some threat. I was sure she'd be in a terrible mood.

As I waited, I heard a sniff. I looked round at her.

She was crying.

I was completely unprepared for this situation. So I did the first thing that came to mind: I ignored her and went straight to the *barre*.

I heard Ivy say, quietly, "Are you... all right, Penny?"

Penny said nothing, but I could still hear her gulping and sniffing.

Ivy came over and joined me. When I looked at her questioningly she just shrugged, clearly none the wiser.

It wasn't long before Miss Finch noticed. "What's wrong, Penny?" she asked.

"V-Violet," she sobbed. "I just... It's so awful..."

I watched in the mirror as Miss Finch went to her and started talking to her so quietly that I couldn't hear.

I leant over to Ivy, who was practising fourth position. "I didn't know Penny had a heart," I said. "I assumed she was some sort of demon."

Ivy swiped me on the arm. "*Scarlet*," she chastised. "She may have nearly killed her best friend, but it wasn't exactly on purpose. I know we hate her, but shouldn't we give her a break?"

Maybe she had a point. I turned sideways and lifted my leg up to the *barre*. "I think you're underestimating Penny."

"Oh? And how am I doing that?"

"You're assuming she's crying because she's sad and feels guilty. I think you're wrong. Little miss *perfect*

186

prefect has just been punished. I think she's crying because she's *angry*."

Chapter Twenty-Two

IVY

It wasn't until the following evening that Ariadne came knocking frantically at our dorm room door, the Whispers' book in her hands. She threw it down on my bed triumphantly.

"Done," she said. "I never want to look at that blasted thing again!"

She proceeded to flop on to the carpet.

"You worked out all of it?" asked Scarlet. She actually seemed a little impressed.

Ariadne beamed at her. "The whole thing," she said.

I peered at her from the edge of my bed. "Are you all right, Ariadne?"

"No. I was up half the night with Rose, and the other half staring at numbers. To begin with I thought that A was one and B was two and so on, but that just gave me words like 'DZOOH'. But then I wondered if the second word might be 'WHISPERS', like the title on the book, which meant that '4' means W. Which is the fourth letter from the *end* of the alphabet."

"You mean—"

"Yes, it's just the alphabet running backwards instead of forwards. Took me half the night to work it out, and it's so simple! Here, please just take it off me."

Well, I was eager to read it. I picked up the book and opened it at the first page. Ariadne had gone through the whole thing, writing the letters underneath as she translated the code. The first page read, perhaps unsurprisingly:

7-19-22
T-H-E
4-19-18-8-11-22-9-8
W-H-I-S-P-E-R-S
18-13
I-N

7-19-22

T-H-E

4-26-15-15-8

W-A-L-L-S

"Did you read it?" Scarlet asked Ariadne, who was staring despondently at the ceiling.

"Not exactly," she said. "But I got the gist of it. And I don't want to read it again, thank you very much."

Scarlet scooted over on to my bed and together we began to read through the book.

It took us some time to read it all, with me having to wait for Scarlet, her nudging me when she wanted me to turn the page. But when we we'd finished, I realised exactly why Ariadne was reacting the way she was – and it wasn't just exhaustion or the tedium of cracking the code.

"I can't believe it," I said. "I never thought..."

The book was a list of all the things that the girls knew or suspected about Mr Bartholomew, and it did *not* make for comfortable reading. It named him at the beginning before referring to him simply as 'he' from then on.

He favours daughters of his rich friends.
He fired a teacher for giving one of them bad marks.
He locked a teacher in a cupboard all night for refusing

to punish a pupil.

He makes pupils run around the school until they collapse.

He stood by while a girl had an asthma attack when she was exhausted from running.

He makes rule-breakers swim laps of the lake in the dark.

He gave one girl such a beating that he broke her arm.

All of this, and more. The list went on and on, each entry more horrifying than the last. Even though Mr Bartholomew was now a frail old man, he was still terrifying – so I could well imagine he was capable of all of this. I felt sick with fear and disgust.

The last line made both of us gasp. The handwriting changed, and the writer gave up on the code halfway through writing.

26-02-14

A – Y – M? That can't be right...

The whispers have been silenced. We have witnessed a catastrophe. This man is even more dangerous than we thought. We must lie low for a while. I am too afraid to speak any further.

I looked up at Scarlet, watched her face as she read those words. Her brow furrowed and her mouth opened into a puzzled O.

Finally she looked up at me. "What on earth? What could... what could be worse than *that*?" She waved her hand over the book, and I knew what she meant. Something worse than corrupt behaviour, than cruelty and beatings and suffering?

"If this is true... Mr Bartholomew makes Miss Fox look tame," I said. Scarlet glared at me. "Well, I know what she did to you and Violet was truly, truly awful but this is... this is the *whole school* we're talking about."

"No," she said, "it's not that. It's that he's *getting away with it*. He's still here! What if he starts doing it all again?"

"What if he already has?" asked Ariadne, her voice wavering.

She had a point. I'd been made to run around the school in the pouring rain. And maybe we'd been fortunate enough not to be discovered breaking any major rules yet, but what about those who had? What had he done to Penny and Nadia?

Scarlet jumped up, and I could almost see the anger bursting through her veins. "We have to stop him," she said. "What if he actually does think I'm the thief? There's no telling what he'd do! He's sick and twisted!"

"There might be more," said Ariadne.

"More what?" Scarlet snapped.

"More evidence. I mean, it said it on the wall, didn't it? *Collect evidence of the truth.* That means they might have had proof of what he'd done."

"We searched that whole room, though," I said. "And there was nowhere else to hide anything. The book was all there was."

Scarlet was stomping around now, the way she always did when she was in this mood. I knew that the worst thing for making her angry was when there was a situation she could do nothing about. "We'll hunt for more evidence," she said firmly. "But even if we find nothing, we're going to discover what this catastrophe was, and we *are* going to bring him to justice."

I smiled a little despite myself. Mr Bartholomew was a formidable force, but he was going to regret messing with Scarlet Grey.

As my twin slammed the little book shut, something fluttered to the ground.

I picked it up. It was a scrap of newspaper, the corner of a page – just the word 'GIRL' in big letters and a date. My twin frowned at it. "Do you think that's another clue?" she asked.

"Look," Ariadne said, leaning over my shoulder and

excitedly jabbing her finger at the scrap. "*26-02-1914.*
That's what was written in the book. I thought it was more
code, but it's a date!"

"A *meaningless* date," my twin added. "We weren't even
alive then. How are we supposed to find out what any of this
means?"

Ariadne smiled. "Where there's a way, there's a way!"

"I don't think that's how the phrase goes, Ariadne,"
I said.

Chapter Twenty-Three

SCARLET

I should have kept a low profile while snooping for clues. But Penny Winchester got in the way, as usual. She pushed past me as we filed into ballet class the next day.

"Hey!" I snapped. *What was she playing at?*

She said nothing and just sat down on the floorboards, lacing on her pointe shoes. I glared at her.

She's crying because she's angry. My own words replayed in my head.

In the *adagio* portion of the lesson, we had to practise an *arabesque*. Miss Finch said the turnout of my hip was nearly perfect.

Next, she appraised Penny. "Not bad," she said, head to one side, "but I fear you've rather lost your technique. Make sure you're keeping everything straight."

I beamed at myself in the mirror as I rose on to my toe to do the move *en pointe*. Suddenly, someone kicked me in the back of the leg and I went tumbling to the ground.

For a moment, I was in shock, not sure what had happened. Then I looked up and saw Penny, trying to cover her laughter with her hand. Other girls were staring down at me like I was some sort of freak, sprawled on the floor of the studio.

Oh no. I am not *having this*, I thought. *I am* not *going to let her think she can mess with me again.*

Typical Penny, full of amusement at what she'd done, preened her beloved blue bow into place.

So I climbed to my feet, reached out, and snatched the bow right out of her hair.

"Give that back!" she yelled, suddenly not enjoying the game any more.

I gave her a wry smile, and ripped the bow in two.

I held out my hands and uncurled them. A scrap of material fell out of each and fluttered slowly to the floor, trailing strands of copper hair. There was a murmured commotion from behind me as the other girls realised what was happening.

"You *witch*," Penny hissed at me. "My daddy gave me that. How dare you?"

Ivy grabbed hold of my arm. "Scarlet, stop it," she warned in my ear, but I shook her off.

"Haven't you learnt to stay away from me yet, Winchester?" I said. "I don't care if the king of England gave you the stupid thing. It's obviously not helping you to be less of a moron, so you don't need it."

Penny glared at me, her mouth hanging open.

"Maybe you should just drop out of ballet class after all, Penny! You'll never be as good as me, PENNY!"

"Shut up," she said. "ShutupshutupSHUTUP!"

I shrugged at her. Every nerve I hit was another victory. "You just can't take the truth, can you?"

Ivy was trying her best to drag me away now, but I had started and I wouldn't stop until I'd finished. "You know what? I know what you're afraid of. You're afraid that Violet likes *me* more than you. Because she has said more than two words to me since she got back. But Violet thinks I'm the worst scum of the earth – and now *you* nearly killed her. So what *must* she think of you?"

And with that, Penny hit me square in the jaw.

"Girls!" Miss Finch shouted. I'd never heard her properly

shout before. "Stop this right away!"

I clutched my cheek, a burning pain radiating across my face. Clumsily I tried to swing back at her, but Miss Finch came between us, and I missed by a mile.

"Penny, Scarlet!" she shouted again. "What are you doing?"

"She kicked me!" I yelled back, at the same time as Penny roared, "She tore up my bow!"

Miss Finch's nostrils flared. "Right. Penny, over there." She pointed to the far corner of the room. "Scarlet, over there. Now." She pointed to the opposite corner.

"But Miss!" we both protested.

"Now!" she repeated. I slunk over to my corner, nursing my jaw.

"Both of you will stay here after class and explain to me *exactly* what you thought you were doing. Until then, you will sit in silence and face the wall, understand?"

"Yes, *Miss*," I said, plonking myself down on the floor. Penny didn't speak.

Great. Another punishment.

But I risked a smile at myself in the mirror. The memory of Penny's horrified face was enough to make it worth it.

Or at least, it was, until class ended and Mr Bartholomew walked in.

I heard his horrible shuffling footsteps before I saw his face.

Miss Finch had left us sitting in silence before giving us a telling off, no doubt to let us stew a little longer.

He approached her at the piano. "Afternoon," he said.

"Good afternoon, sir," she replied, her voice somewhat squeakier than normal.

"I've come to speak with you about some financial matters. Ones that have arisen after – oh." He stopped, and slowly swivelled his head in my direction. I held my breath, feeling his gaze boring into the back of my head. Then he turned and noticed Penny. "Have these students misbehaved?"

Say no, I pleaded silently. *Tell him everything's fine. Tell him we just enjoy sitting in corners, for goodness' sake.*

Unfortunately, he took Miss Finch's loyal silence as a yes.

He stifled a cough. "Mmhmm. And have you assigned a suitable punishment?"

I felt a chill run down my spine.

"Well, I thought I would give them some lines," she said weakly. "Or perhaps an essay on proper behaviour."

The headmaster shook his head. "Oh no, that won't do," he drawled. "You see, Miss Finch, students are fickle creatures. They will say that they have learnt from a punishment, that they'll never do it again. Perhaps... perhaps some of it may even enter their minds. But it's not *permanent*."

He stared at me again, and I wished over and over that I

199

had the guts to get up and run. But for some reason I stayed sitting on the cold floor, not daring to move a muscle.

"It is important when providing discipline," he carried on in his nasty rattling voice, "that we give the students something memorable. And I can already see that my previous efforts in Miss Winchester's case were not... sufficient."

I heard Penny gasp behind me. My stomach turned over as my imagination conjured up the horrors that could be inflicted on us.

"I assure you," said Miss Finch, and I saw her try to drag herself up to his height in the reflection, "I will deal with the situation accordingly."

I couldn't breathe. Would he buy that? Every second that passed increased my panic.

Please believe her. Please. Please.

Mr Bartholomew's voice lowered to almost a whisper, but it echoed off the walls of the ballet studio and seeped into my ears. "See that you do. Or their punishment will become yours. I WILL have discipline in this school!"

Chapter Twenty-Four

Ivy

When Scarlet returned to our room that afternoon, she was shaking.

"What were you playing at?" I demanded, as soon as she walked in. "The last thing we needed was for you to get in trouble again!"

She didn't reply, just walked straight past me.

"Come on, Scarlet," I said. "We've got bigger things to worry about than your petty squabbles with Penny. You need to learn to ignore her!" It was a bit rich coming from me, I know – when I'd been acting at being Scarlet, I hadn't done a great job of ignoring Penny, either.

But Scarlet looked up at me, and there was something in her eyes that I wasn't used to seeing: fear. "He came to the ballet studio," she said flatly.

"Who did?" I asked, but I had a horrible feeling that I already knew the answer.

"Mr Bartholomew. Started talking about how we needed a *memorable punishment*." She grimaced. "All I could think about was that he was going to beat me or... or lock Penny and I up... in *there*..." As her voice quavered, I realised that the second part was what Scarlet feared most.

My irritation melted away as I began to feel sorry for my twin again. "How did you get away?"

"Miss Finch stood up to him. I can't believe it. She told him she'd discipline us herself. I just... I didn't think he'd accept it. I thought he would force her to make us do something awful."

I sat down on my bed. "So what did she actually do?"

"She just went very quiet, and then told us to write an essay for homework. Then she sent us out."

"Goodness. Sounds like you really dodged a bullet there."

"That doesn't make me feel much better," she snapped. "He can't get away with this! It's just like the Whispers said. What if it's happening all over again?"

I frowned at her. "Well, then now would be a good time to stop breaking rules, wouldn't it?"

Scarlet was right, though, and that worried me. We needed to find more of the evidence against Mr Bartholomew before something awful happened.

"I think we should go to the nurse, and see if she'll let us talk to Violet," I said, as we made our way down to dinner. "Yes, she's awful, but what if she knows something? Or Rose! What if Rose knows something?"

Scarlet wrinkled her nose. "What could that be? How to lurk about and not talk to people?"

"She *lives* in that secret room. She must know every inch of it by now."

"Do you really fancy another night-time excursion, knowing what Mr Bartholomew might do to us? I'm sending Ariadne."

I didn't respond to that.

We picked up trays and joined the back of the dinner queue. I spotted Ariadne at the other side of the hall and waved her over.

"How's life without the blood-sucking fiend?" Scarlet asked her. I whacked her on the arm.

"About the same. Still quiet. I think Rose misses her, though."

"How could anyone miss Violet?" Scarlet asked.

"Ahem." Someone cleared their throat.

"I mean, she's so *strange*. And possibly evil."

"Shut up, Scarlet," I said.

"AHEM!"

I turned to the kitchen hatch to see the cook standing there, hands on her hips. "When you've finished chin-wagging, you can take your food!" she barked.

"Oh. Sorry."

The food was slices of some kind of roast meat in a watery gravy, buried under mashed potatoes and wilted cabbage that looked like it had only had a brief glimpse of the sun before being tugged out of the ground. I pulled a face at it as I took my tray over to the Richmond table. Ariadne and Scarlet followed close behind me.

Ariadne seemed unusually quiet, and she was ignoring her food. But she had her thinking face on. "What is it?" I asked.

"I just keep thinking about that message, you know..." She lowered her voice so I could just hear her over the dining hall din. "*We witnessed a catastrophe.* I just can't imagine..."

She was interrupted by the sound of Scarlet slapping herself on the forehead.

"What?" Ariadne and I said in unison.

"Miss Jones!" Scarlet exclaimed. "That's her name!"

I stared at my twin, wondering what the heck she was on about. "What's her name?"

"Cassie. Short for... *Catastrophe*."

"That's an odd name," Ariadne said.

"As if you can talk," said Scarlet. "Besides, it's true. She told me. And if it's true, that means the Whispers were trying to tell us something. About her."

My friend's face screwed up in puzzlement. "*Witnessed...*" She tried. "Witnessed! Catastrophe witnessed!" She'd said it a little too loudly, earning a disapproving look from Mrs Knight.

We all quietened down after that, and attempted to chew whatever the meat was. But I knew that all of our brains were whirring. So Miss Jones might have been at the school back then, and she might have witnessed – well, whatever it was that was so awful.

But all I could think was – if someone had the chance to leave the horrors of Rookwood... Why on earth would they come back?

When dinner was over, we headed straight for the library. If this really was a clue, we had to look into it.

"We need to ask Miss Jones about the newspaper," Ariadne said excitedly, as we hurried along the hallway. "They might have it in the archives."

I agreed with her. "If we ask her about whatever this event was, she might be too scared to talk. Or she might flip and get us in trouble—"

"But finding the newspaper might tell us all we need to know." Scarlet slapped Ariadne on the back, causing her to nearly spit out the boiled sweet she was sucking. "Brilliant!" Ariadne looked pleased, despite being winded.

It wasn't long until bedtime, so there was only a handful of girls milling about in the library. We found Miss Jones sitting in front of the grand fireplace, warming her hands on the crackling hearth. "Oh, hello, girls," she said. She sounded nervous. "I was just getting a bit chilly, you know."

I wasn't entirely sure why she was explaining herself – the windows were frosted over and the air was brisk. We could all feel it. Standing by the fire was the first time I'd felt truly warm all day.

"This school has always been quite cold, hasn't it?" I asked. "Even in... the old days?"

She gave me a puzzled look. "I... suppose so? It was when I was a pupil here." *Aha!* "Well, anyway, I must get back to work! It's important to work hard," she said, picking up a stack of books that she'd balanced on a chair.

We looked at each other. Why was she acting so oddly? "Has anything else gone missing?" Scarlet asked.

"I don't think so," Miss Jones replied. She gave a fevered

glance at the ceiling. "I wish I could hang around. But I can't. I have tidying and cataloguing to do. And I must make sure that I leave on time." She hurried away, the stack of books rocking in her arms.

"He's got to her," said Scarlet with a frown. "He must have done."

I was ready to give up, but I should've known that my twin wouldn't be so easily put off. She was already chasing after the librarian.

"Miss! We've got an assignment, actually."

"Oh?" There was a faraway look in Miss Jones's eyes. "What's it for?"

"Local history," she lied. "We've got to find an old newspaper."

"Ah!" The librarian's face brightened a little, obviously keen to have something to do that she could be certain was work. "Of course. Just over here."

She led us over to the archives, and deposited her stack of books on the floor.

The newspapers were held in large leather-bound volumes, stacked up along the shelves with the year printed on the side. I stood on tiptoes to read the plaque at the top: *The Richmond Gazette*. "So these are all the local newspapers?"

"Yes, going back a hundred years or so. Which one was it you wanted?"

I nudged my twin, and she produced the scrap of paper from her pocket. "The twenty-sixth of February, nineteen fourteen."

The date didn't seem to trigger any sort of recognition in the librarian. She just ran a finger along the rows until she came to the book marked '1914'. She retrieved it and balanced it on her knee, having to blow some of the dust off it first. Then she tipped it open and rifled through. "February, February... ah, here we go. That's funny, someone has torn the corner off."

I took the yellowed paper out of her hands. And I knew instantly which article we were looking for.

DROWNS IN FREAK SCHOOL ACCIDENT

Chapter Twenty-Five

SCARLET

I tried to press down the emotions that bubbled up and to keep my face totally blank. Ivy and Ariadne didn't do so well – they looked like they were about to be sick.

"That one," I said, pointing at it. "That's the one."

Miss Jones appeared not to even register the horrific headline; I supposed she hadn't read it.

"You girls will look after this, won't you? Don't take it out of the library. You can spend ten minutes with it now and then you'll have to come back tomorrow." She replaced the volume in the archive and then picked up her stack of books again. "So much to do…"

Before we could say anything else, she had wandered away, leaving us staring down at the newspaper. If she knew something, it was going to be difficult getting it out of her.

"This is it," I said. "We need to read this." Scarlet nodded briskly, wide-eyed.

We headed for a nearby table. But just as we did so, I heard a familiar dry, hacking cough. Quickly, I pulled the others out of sight behind a bookshelf and we peered back round and watched as Mr Bartholomew greeted the librarian.

"H-h-h-hello, Headmaster," she replied. She sounded terrified. Was every adult in this school intimidated by Mr Bartholomew?

"Ah… Miss Jones. I'm just making my rounds to check no misdemeanours are taking place. I trust the library is a haven of quiet and study?"

"O-of course! I was showing some pupils the newspaper archives just now – such keen students of local history…"

I wasn't sticking around to get caught by him. All three of us ducked under the table and hid there until he had left. Then I placed the torn-off corner back against the page – it fitted perfectly. We read…

GIRL DROWNS IN FREAK SCHOOL ACCIDENT

Tragedy struck at the prestigious Rookwood School last night, as a pupil (15) was discovered drowned on the shore of the estate's lake this morning. Distressed fellow students reported seeing something floating in the water and teachers were swiftly alerted. The deceased has not yet been named and little is known about her, but it is believed that her death was the result of a night-swimming escapade gone badly wrong.

An Anonymous Teacher commented thusly: "We are all deeply saddened by the unfortunate loss of life here at Rookwood. Rest assured that we are doing all we can to ensure that this does not happen again. Parents do not need to panic, this was clearly an unforeseeable accident, and we want to reassure them that their daughters are perfectly safe in our hands." She added that a plaque would be erected on the school grounds, in memory of the student.

Headmaster Edgar Bartholomew declined to speak to *The Richmond Gazette* at this time.

I turned my head to look at my twin. "I bet I know what happened," I said. "It wasn't an accident. Well, not the kind they think it was."

"What do you mean?" asked Ivy.

"He probably *made* her do it! He made her go swimming in the lake at night, as a punishment! That's why he wouldn't talk to the reporter!" I clenched my hand into a fist.

"This is what the Whispers meant," said Ariadne. I nodded. Ivy put her hand over her mouth. She had finally seen what I was getting at.

And I wondered: had Miss Jones been a pupil here at the beginning of 1914? And could she have seen it happen?

It was *sickening*. He'd more than gone too far. Mr Bartholomew had *killed* someone. His obsession with discipline had resulted in a pupil's death and terrified the Whispers into silence.

And I was *not* going to let him get away with it. Scarlet was about ready to run to the headmaster's office and beat him around the head with the newspaper. That, or personally call the police and demand his arrest. It took Ariadne and I some time to talk her out of it, until Miss Jones reappeared and asked us to replace the newspaper and head to bed.

As Ariadne slunk back to her dorm, I turned to Scarlet. She'd finally calmed down a little.

"We need evidence," I said, for what felt like the fifth time. "Otherwise nobody's going to believe us."

She didn't look at me. "Why not the code book?"

"We could have just written that ourselves. And we can't

exactly show off the secret room, can we? If they find out what Miss Finch did, she'll be fired. We need to look after Rose."

"Speak for yourself. I don't see why I have to look after her."

I glared at her. "It's *your* turn tonight!"

That got her to look up. "I'm not going on my own. Mr Bartholomew could catch me and have me torn to pieces and fed to the rooks."

Although she was being ridiculous, the thought made me pause. *Can't lose her again...*

"Fine, I'll go with you. But just to make sure you don't get yourself into any more trouble."

Chapter Twenty-Six

Ivy

It was earlier at night than we usually ventured out, but it had been a freezing cold day (Scarlet had refused to take off her coat and scarf) and I was getting worried about Rose. It was still late enough that the teachers would all be at home in their beds.

Ariadne joined us and the darkness swept over us as we all crept down the stairs. A sudden noise as we passed one of the tall windows made me jump, but it was just an owl hooting in the night.

I stifled a yawn, wishing that I were curled up in bed.

My twin seemed on even higher alert than usual. I didn't blame her – I could almost imagine Mr Bartholomew stalking behind us, shuffling along, his breathing creaking like an open door in the wind. Was he really always watching?

As we tiptoed through the school, I imagined I could hear the victims of the headmaster's years of terror. Crying out. Begging for their stories to be told.

The girl whose arm had been broken. Did her parents know? Did Mr Bartholomew tell them she'd hurt herself in a fall?

The teacher who'd been locked in a cupboard all night. Did she bang on the door and scream, waiting to be let out? Was she frightened?

The girl who'd been forced to run around the school until she'd suffered an asthma attack. Had anyone believed her?

These people went round and round in my head until I felt dizzy.

I promised myself that I wouldn't forget them. I carried the book with me, hoping to stash it in the hidden room, where it would be safe.

And that was when we saw the shadow. It flickered and grew larger, looming up the wall. There were heavy footsteps on the wooden floor.

We quickly pushed open the moving bookcase and

dashed inside.

It was probably a rat, I told myself.

An *enormous* rat.

Rose was sitting on her makeshift bed, reading one of the pony books that Violet had given her and eating a bar of chocolate, some of which had smudged on to her cheeks. She was half-buried under a pile of blankets, and she'd plaited her blonde hair into a braid. She looked up as we walked in and smiled.

"Are you all right?" I asked her, handing her a fresh mug of water that I'd brought from upstairs. She nodded and took the mug, drinking gratefully.

"I don't know how she can live down here," said Scarlet, scuffing her foot against the floor.

I gave my twin a Look. "Just because Rose doesn't talk much, doesn't mean she doesn't have ears. And besides, she doesn't have a choice."

Rose looked up at me, but her eyes gave nothing away. She seemed fine, but it couldn't have been nice, in the cold and the dark. Even with all the candles. We couldn't keep her down here forever.

We sat there in her quiet company for a while, trying to stop our teeth chattering, until suddenly we heard footsteps on the stairs. I jumped up, worried. They sounded heavy.

Oh no. That shadow I'd seen. Was it him? Had Mr Bartholomew been lurking outside all this time?

Scarlet jumped up too, and took my hand. There was nowhere to run. Whoever this was, we had to face them together.

A figure staggered into the room, laden with blankets. To my surprise, it was Violet. She looked as astonished to see as us we were to see her.

"Violet! What are you doing down here?"

"I've sneaked down from the sick bay," she explained, rushing to Rose and draping another woollen blanket around her tiny shoulders. "Nurse Gladys is going to let me out tomorrow, so it was my last chance to smuggle these out and bring them down here."

Rose stared up at her happily. "Hello, Miss Violet," she said.

"You're just in time," I said. "It's freezing. I don't know if she'd have survived the night down here without the extra warmth."

"Well, I'm back now," said Violet briskly. "You can leave her with me. I rescued her from the asylum, so I can look after her."

I frowned. Didn't she remember what Miss Finch had said?

Scarlet was furious. "Don't I even get a thank you for

hauling you out of the lake? I could have been pulled into the water myself! Or what about looking after your little pet while you've been recovering? Of all the ungrateful..."

"Miss Violet..."

"Scarlet Grey, if you think I'm *ever* going to thank you after all this, then..."

"Miss Violet!"

That stopped everyone in their tracks. We all looked at Rose. Here eyes were fixed on the doorway we'd entered through. "They're here," she said.

"Rose, what are you—" Violet started.

We all turned.

Someone was there.

It was Penny.

Chapter Twenty-Seven

Ivy

The expression on Penny's face was one of pure fury.

"What are you doing?" Her voice was flat, her eyes narrowed.

To my surprise, Violet started babbling. "Penny, listen, it's nothing, I'll explain, don't..."

"No," said Penny, and she stood firm as a rock. "What is this?" She got louder. "What are you doing with *them*?"

I looked round. Ariadne had her hand over her mouth

and had gone pale as porridge. Scarlet looked like she was considering violence. I grabbed her hand pre-emptively.

"It's nothing," repeated Violet, and she stepped forward, her arms raised in a defensive gesture.

Penny merely swiped them away. She was out for blood. "*No*," she repeated. "You do *not* do this to me. You do not just sneak around with these *losers* in the dead of night and then lie to me about it! You've only just got out of the sick bay, and you haven't even spoken to me yet! I tried to find you in the nurse's office to APOLOGISE, but you'd disappeared AGAIN!"

"You were the one who put me in there," Violet replied. You could taste the acid in her voice.

"That's irrelevant," said Penny, although I was pretty sure it wasn't. "I searched around the school for you. Then I swear I see you slipping into the library, and I find this bookcase that swings open and it's ajar and there's a secret passage and..." She stopped, almost too furious to go on. "This is madness! Tell me what you're doing and tell me who the heck this girl is, right now!" She flung out her arm and pointed, her chest rising and falling as if it could barely contain her anger.

And then, with the worst possible timing, Rose stood up. The blankets fell loosely around her.

"AND WHY IS SHE WEARING MY CLOTHES?"

Penny screamed.

"I rescued her," said Violet. "From the asylum. Please, Penny, I'll do anything, just don't tell..."

"Don't tell the headmaster?!" Penny yelled back. And then she suddenly froze. We all stared at her. The candlelight glinted off her golden prefect badge.

"Oh no," I whispered.

And before I could even move, Penny turned on her heels and ran.

"NO!" Violet shouted, and in seconds she was giving chase. And then I was running too, and I prayed that Scarlet and Ariadne were behind me. We couldn't let Mr Bartholomew find out about Rose – even more than that, we couldn't let him find out that we were involved. As I ran to the stairs, flashes of his hideous punishments sparked in my head.

But Penny was fast, and she had shot a way up the spiral staircase before we even got there. Violet lunged up through a gap in the wood and grabbed her ankle, but Penny kicked like a donkey and threw her off.

"Penny!" I yelled up at her. "Stop this! We can sort something out!"

My words had no effect. She had already hurled her weight at the moving bookcase and tumbled out. I heard thundering footsteps on the stairs behind me, but I didn't look back. We needed to catch her. Violet was already slowing, her breathing ragged.

We raced through the bookshelves, Penny's copper hair whipping out behind her as she ran. I didn't shout again, dreading the thought of someone hearing us. Faster and faster, out of the library doors, along the corridor. She was getting nearer to his office, and every frantic step made my heart beat faster.

Please, I begged silently. *Please don't be in there. Please be at home in bed.*

To my horror, Penny skidded to a halt, and began hammering her fists on the office door. "Sir!" she yelled. "Sir!"

We were too late.

I stopped, caught my breath. Violet was beside me, and she sank down to her knees.

Penny knocked with all her might, but I sensed an air of desperation. The door remained firmly shut.

I walked over to her. She wouldn't stop hitting the door. Without hesitation, I grabbed her wrists. Her fists were raw, and she started to cry.

"I hate you," she sobbed. "I hate you all. I will tell him! I will!" She choked back the tears and wiped her face on her nightgown.

Violet hadn't even looked up. She was staring at the floor.

It was like she had just shut down.

Scarlet and Ariadne appeared behind her. Ariadne stopped when she saw that nothing was happening, and leant forward with her hands on her knees as she attempted to regain her breath. But Scarlet marched over to where I was standing with Penny.

"Who do you think you are?" she demanded, giving Penny a firm shove in the chest. Penny stumbled back, tears still streaming down her face.

"I'm... I'm doing what's right," Penny said. Her fists were clenched. "You've broken *all* the rules!"

"Oh, so you're a saint now, are you?" snapped my sister. "Saving everyone from our wicked misdemeanours? YOU pushed Violet in the lake, and now you're punishing her for having the audacity to leave you out of something!"

"Who cares?" Penny snapped back. "I'm not letting you get away with it either way! I'll find Mr Bartholomew tomorrow and tell him, I'll..."

My twin grabbed her by the collar. "Listen here, you little weasel. What makes you think he's even going to believe you?"

But Penny had hold of her arm and I watched as she slowly dug her nails into Scarlet's skin. "Let. Go. Of. Me."

Scarlet stood still, her grip remaining solid. But the sharp fingernails sank deeper. She began to wince, and the wince turned to a grimace. She shook her arm away. "Fine! Fine. But you can answer the question."

"I'm a prefect," Penny sniffed. "Of course he'll believe me." But even she didn't look that convinced by her own words. She leant back against the heavy door, defeated.

I breathed a sigh of relief, for the moment at least. We'd bought ourselves time. We could get Miss Finch to move Rose somewhere, get rid of the proof that she'd been there. We could tell Mr Bartholomew that Penny was making the whole thing up, that she had a known vendetta against Scarlet and had fallen out with Violet – even pushing Violet into the lake hadn't been enough revenge for her.

"Can you smell smoke?" Ariadne said suddenly.

I sniffed the air. It *did* smell of smoke. Where was it coming from?

"One of you circus freaks probably knocked over a candle," Penny sneered through her tears.

I looked at Scarlet in horror. Together we went and peered back around the corner. Smoke was billowing violently from the vast doors.

The library was on fire.

Chapter Twenty-Eight

SCARLET

"Oh my god," I said.

Ivy turned back. "Fire," she whispered. And then louder, "There's a fire!"

Ariadne flapped her arms. "We've got to fetch someone!" she said. "Or get everyone out! Or both! Oh no, oh no..."

"ROSE!" Violet shouted. She'd snapped out of it, and before I could stop her she was up and running past us into the library. This was *not* good.

I ran after her.

"Scarlet, don't!" Ivy begged, terror in her voice.

"Get help!" was my only response.

As I ran back into the vast room, I saw just how *not good* it was. The fire was raging, a seething orange and yellow mass flickering its way across the shelves. The smoke was threatening to choke me. I wrapped my scarf around my face and ran on. "Violet!" I yelled after her, hoping to slow her down.

"The secret door!" she called back, panic-stricken, and I realised with dismay what she meant. The moving bookcase must be on fire.

I pulled the scarf down from my mouth for a second. "Go the other way!" I tilted my head. Violet leapt into action, and she was beside me as we sprinted down the rows of books.

The fire was spreading quickly. I could see the moving bookcase, and it was burning, pages curling up from the books as the flames ate away at them, flecks of white floating up to the ceiling. The heat was intense.

All my senses were telling me to get out of there. *But Rose...*

"How can we get in?" Violet gasped, tears streaming from her eyes. The smoke stung mine as well, and I tried to pull the scarf up further.

I thought faster than I'd ever thought in my life. "We

need to try and bash straight through it. Ladder," I said, my hand snapping out.

There was a short ladder on wheels nearby, used for reaching the higher shelves. Violet didn't have to be told twice. She took one end and I took the other, and we carried it towards the secret door. We were so near the fire now that the heat was almost unbearable.

Something crunched under my feet. I looked down. *Glass?* And then I saw it. The oil lamp was on the floor, smashed open and engulfed in flames.

We had to get Rose, and time was running out.

"Now!" I called.

Violet and I rammed the ladder into the door and it swung round, still on fire. And then we were both through the gap, coughing and steaming. I patted myself down quickly – none of my clothes had caught.

Violet shot off down the staircase. All thoughts of being quiet forgotten, she yelled Rose's name over and over.

We found her at the bottom, staring upwards. "Rose," Violet said, breathless, "we have to go, quick, there's a fire."

Rose nodded her understanding.

I tried to take her hand, but she suddenly swerved away from me and back into her room.

"Rose!" Violet called after her. But within seconds she was back, and she'd retrieved something.

It was the book of pony stories.

We ran back up the stairs. They creaked ominously under our weight. The smoke increased as we neared the top, a big grey cloud that threatened to choke us. I soon saw why – the fire was spreading to the staircase.

The top of it had already caught, and was slowly creeping along. The step and the banister wouldn't resist it for long, I knew that.

"No, no, no!" Violet cried.

"We have to jump!" I said, but my words were muffled by my scarf. The doorway was still clear, but for how much longer?

And just as I thought that, one of the top shelves collapsed into the gap, making it even smaller. Burning books tumbled to the ground, crackling.

Violet flung herself forward and leapt through the tight space. I watched with horror as her sleeve caught fire, but she rolled forward on to the floor, over and over, until it was out.

I braced myself to move, but I soon realised that Violet had left Rose behind. The poor girl stood there, coughing and crying in the acrid smoke, still gripping her book.

Pulling down my scarf as much as I could bear, I looked her in the eye. "Rose, we need to get through there. Can I take your hand?"

As soon as she nodded, I seized her hand, and we jumped.

Using Violet's trick, I pulled her down to the hard floor, and we both rolled away from the fire. I felt my eyebrows and hair singe.

In a daze, I staggered back to my feet. I knew Rose was beside me, and I knew we had to get out. But my throat was raw, and my head was spinning.

Together we stumbled forward across the library.

There was an alarm, a bell. So loud. *The fire alarm!* Someone had rung it!

Not far to go.

Through blurry vision I saw the vast doors of the library. I sped up, dragging Rose along beside me. My lungs felt tight and painful, the pressure inside them was intense...

Violet. She stood by the door, panting, retching. I grabbed her too. Every step we took was a step further away from the smoke, closer to freedom.

Around. *Not far.* Along the corridor. *Nearly there.* I kept repeating it to myself. The bell went *clangclangclang* in my ears.

Suddenly there was a swarm of girls in nightgowns. *Evacuating*, I realised. They flowed into the entrance hall and we were swept along with them.

The doors were wide open, and I felt the cold, cold air

on my face.

We stepped out, Violet and Rose and I. Stepped into the freezing night, the whole school behind us.

We'd made it. We were alive.

I fell forward into the snow.

Chapter Twenty-Nine

Ivy

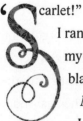carlet!"

I ran forward, and I couldn't keep the tears from my eyes. *Scarlet. My twin.* Her clothes were blackened, her hair singed at the ends.

No. I won't lose her again.

I turned her over and shook her shoulders. "Scarlet, wake up! Wake up!"

After a few long, painful moments, her head rolled back, and she started to cough.

The fire alarm Ariadne had set off rang in my ears.

Other girls were crowding around us on the gravel, staring, whispering.

"Get back," Ariadne said. "Shoo!" She waved them away. "Teacher! We need a teacher! Help!"

Scarlet coughed more, and then, finally, her eyes snapped open. "What... what happened?" she asked, gulping down the fresh air.

"Oh, Scarlet," was all I could say, and I swept her into a hug.

"Not too tight," she murmured. I leant back from her. There was soot all down my front.

A stout figure hurried down the school steps; the matron, I realised, in the glow of the lamppost. Her hair was still rolled up in curlers, and she was wearing a thick housecoat. "I've telephoned the fire brigade," she called breathlessly. "Just stay calm girls! Huddle together for warmth!"

Everyone was in their nightgowns, and I'd forgotten for a moment how freezing I was. The matron began herding people into groups, enlisting Maureen and Lettie with their shiny prefect badges to help her, and I watched as Ariadne slipped away towards them.

"Can you stand?" I asked Scarlet.

"I think so," she said. She wiped her face with what remained of her scarf, and pulled it down around her neck.

Nadia and her older sister, Meena, pushed through the

crowd. I looked up into Meena's worried face. "Let us help," she said.

I nodded, and Nadia crouched down beside me. Nadia took Scarlet's other shoulder, and together we lifted her upright. The snowflakes clung to my fingers, cold and damp.

Ariadne appeared again, and she had the matron and Nurse Gladys in tow. "Here," she said. "I think she breathed in a lot of smoke."

The two women looked at each other – probably thinking the same thing: why had Scarlet been near the fire? In the library? In the middle of the night?

If they were thinking that, they didn't say anything at that moment. Instead they stepped over and took Scarlet off me and Nadia, and reluctant as I was to let go of her, I knew I had to. The nurse wrapped a blanket around her. As I stood aside, Ariadne took hold of my hand. "She'll be all right," she said.

But I had a question of my own, now. Where had Violet and Rose gone? I'd not seen them come out of the building, but there were so many girls squeezing out of the doors that they would have been easy to miss.

As my eyes searched for them in the crowd, I heard peals of alarm bells in the distance. Help was on its way.

I turned back to Scarlet, who was being fussed over by the nurse and matron. "Did they get out?" I asked quietly. She nodded. *Thank goodness.*

The bells grew louder and louder, until the vehicle came into a view. It was a fire engine, its wheels gripping the salted surface of the drive. Red, shiny, an enormous ladder strapped to the back. It was filled with men in smart buttoned uniforms and metal helmets. I saw them shouting to each other and pointing at the east wing. Some of the library windows had cracked open and smoke was pouring out.

"Stand back, everyone, stand back!" the matron called.

We all moved aside, and watched as the men worked, unfurling a hosepipe from the side of the engine. They began pumping water out of the hose. It sprayed across the windows in an arcing torrent.

Others ran inside, carrying buckets and wearing masks.

"The headmaster has been called," I heard someone say. I wrapped my arms around myself, suddenly succumbing to the cold even more than before.

I couldn't feel my hands and feet, and my teeth were chattering uncontrollably. My friends had stayed close, but it hadn't helped much. At least Scarlet was recovering – her breathing was back to normal, and the spark had returned to her eyes. The nurse said the doctor would arrive soon to examine her and make sure there hadn't been any lasting damage. They still hadn't yet asked what she'd been doing in there.

Mrs Knight arrived. "We'll head for the hall, girls, while

the fire is being dealt with," she said. "We should be safe there on the other side of the school. Walk in pairs, but quickly, please." She wrung her hands together.

In the hall, the staff handed out blankets and someone was sent to brave the kitchens and boil a kettle to make hot tea. We sat on the floor, all shivering together. The usual rabble was absent – everyone was too tired and cold to chatter.

Only Ariadne broke the hush. "Are you all right, Scarlet?"

"Fine, fine," said my twin, but I detected a hint of fear. And I thought I knew why.

"Where's the headmaster?" I overheard the matron muttering to Mrs Knight, as they stood beside us.

"I don't know. We couldn't get hold of him on the telephone, but Gladys said she saw him on the way inside. He'll be here soon," she said, but there was an air of uncertainty to her voice.

And moments later, there he was, trooping into the hall.

Marching Violet and Rose in front of him.

He approached Mrs Knight, his face thunderous. "I found these two *delinquents* trying to hide in the hallway."

"My... my goodness," said Mrs Knight. She peered down at Rose. "Do I know you? Are you a pupil here?"

Rose shook her head.

"She's my friend," said Violet fiercely, before breaking into a hacking cough that rivalled Mr Bartholomew's own.

"She isn't one of ours, sir," Mrs Knight said quietly. "Where did she come from?"

Violet slammed her lips tightly shut, refusing to say another word. And of course, Rose didn't say anything, either.

"They are both covered in soot!" He growled. "These must be our culprits."

Scarlet burrowed down into her blanket, and tipped her head forward so he wouldn't see her face. I didn't have anything to cover up, but I prayed that my clothes didn't smell of smoke.

"There are culprits?" asked the nurse. "You think someone did this deliberately?"

Mr Bartholomew's eyebrows knitted together and he said nothing. He didn't let go of Violet and Rose.

"It could have been an accident, couldn't it?" she said, worry etched in lines on her face. "I should make sure these girls are all right."

Miss Finch came bursting into the hall. "Is everyone safe? What happened?" she cried.

The headmaster stared hard at her, and then at Violet and Rose. "Keep an eye on these two, Miss Finch. Find out who this girl is."

"We've lost everything," Scarlet whispered.

"What?" I asked, leaning closer. Violet and Rose had

been caught, yes, and the library was a casualty, but... there could still be a way out of this. They couldn't prove anything about our involvement.

"The staircase," Scarlet replied absently. "The staircase caught fire. It's probably all gone by now. The wall. The Whispers' book. No way down. "

"Rats," said Ariadne, and I'd never heard her sound so sad.

We all sat there, hanging our heads, pins and needles prickling at our skin as warmth returned. I fought the urge to cry.

The headmaster cleared his throat with that horrible deathly rattle of his.

"Girls," he announced, "it is my hope that the fire will shortly be completely out, and you will be able to return to your beds. Tomorrow's lessons will be cancelled while we investigate this... act of dangerous vandalism."

A shocked murmur rippled out around the hall.

"Silence," he said, and it returned quicker than I could blink.

"I want to make something abundantly clear," he said, and his expression was so malevolent it sent shivers down my spine. "If any of you are found responsible for this fire, it will result in immediate expulsion."

Scarlet raised an eyebrow, and I could tell she was

thinking that it wouldn't be so bad to be kicked out of this hateful school.

But we'd come so close to finding out precious information about our mother, and her involvement in the Whispers. Were we about to be plunged into the dark once more?

Chapter Thirty

SCARLET

We were allowed back to our beds eventually, in the very early hours of the morning, the prefects put in charge of ushering people back to their rooms. I'd had to wait for the nurse to pronounce me fit to leave the hall. I panicked at first, convinced she was going to see how close I'd been to the fire and tell on me. My mind was racing for a good excuse, but Nurse Gladys seemed just as twitchy as the other teachers. She just waved me off and told me to get a good rest, whilst glancing around nervously. Was she afraid of the headmaster too?

I didn't know what would happen to Violet and Rose, but at least for now they were with Miss Finch. How long she would be able to keep them away from the firing line of Mr Bartholomew's questioning, I didn't know.

After washing my face and peeling off my smoke-damaged coat, I fell into bed, numb with exhaustion. My throat felt sore, but my breathing was fine. I drank in the cold air of our room, feeling grateful for it. My lumpy mattress suddenly felt like the most comfortable feather bed in the world.

Just then a horrible realisation hit me. If the fire had destroyed that bit of the bookshelves, it must have destroyed the newspaper archives as well. That newspaper with the report about the drowned pupil would have gone up in smoke. Crushing disappointment filled me. All our evidence had been destroyed. In one fell swoop.

Sleep took a long time to arrive that night.

In my dream, I was on the rooftop, and snow was falling around me.

No. Not snow.

It was ash. Pieces of ash, scraps of paper, twirling through the breeze against a white sky.

I was right on the edge. The world below was so far down, so, so far... but it wasn't the gravel driveway or the grass I saw below me. It was a cage. Hands reached out, grasping the air.

My legs began to shake. I was going to fall.

There was someone behind me, though. Someone calling my name. I whipped around – it was Ivy. She held out her hand to me, and I reached out to her, but I knew something was wrong. Was she too far away?

A shadow crept up behind my twin. It may have been a shadow, but it looked familiar. I recognised it, deep down. It curved over Ivy's shoulders, flowing like smoke, and reached a ghostly hand down into her pocket.

Ivy didn't seem to notice. Her hand remained stretched out towards me, but now she was screaming wordlessly at me, trying to get me to listen.

I looked down at my hands, and they were burning.

I shot upright, panting, sweat on my palms. I examined them quickly, just to make sure they weren't on fire.

Ivy was looking at me sleepily from her bed. The bell hadn't rung this morning. They must have rested it since none of us had any sleep, and it was definitely later than usual. The cold winter sun was already high up in the sky and shining weakly through the window.

I looked at her. "I, uh... bad dream."

She gave me a concerned look, but I didn't elaborate. The dream was too fresh – and had left me feeling puzzled, like there was something I was missing. This school swirled with

241

mysteries, and it seemed their solutions were always just out of reach.

At our late breakfast, all everyone could talk about was the fire.

"I just don't get it," said Ariadne. "It seemed like we were making great progress. And then suddenly there's a fire and it all turns to ash. This is the worst thing that's ever happened."

Ash. Bits of the dream floated through my mind.

"Miss Flitworth?" Mrs Knight approached the table.

Ariadne looked up. "Yes, Miss?"

"Come with me, please."

Ariadne climbed to her feet, slowly, almost forgetting to put down her spoon. Her eyes were wide. "W-what is it?" she asked.

But Mrs Knight said nothing – she simply put a hand on her shoulder and led her away.

Ivy looked at me, panicked. "Why are they taking Ariadne? I mean, she wasn't... you don't think Violet told on her, do you?"

I didn't think so. "That's not her style. If she was going to blame anyone, she'd blame me. I've got singed eyebrows, for goodness' sake! And I had to trim the ends of my hair this morning! I only got away with it because the nurse was shaking with nerves and barely paying attention. Violet could've brought me down easily if she'd pinned the blame on me."

Ivy wasn't reassured. "Something's wrong."

"Something's always wrong," was all I could think to say.

We needed to see what had happened to the library. Then maybe we could figure out what, or who, had started the fire. And we still needed to properly speak to Miss Jones and find out whether she was the Catastrophe mentioned in the Whispers' book.

So I dragged Ivy to the east wing, where we were met with a sad sight: the library doors were chained shut, and someone had added a freshly painted sign that read 'DO NOT ENTER'.

"Oh well," I sighed. "Looks like we're not going to be able to see the damage to the secret door and the newspaper archives. I so hope that newspaper is still there."

Just then we heard someone starting to wail and sob.

We soon located the source. It was Miss Jones, and she was sitting on the floor, hugging her knees to her chest.

"Miss?" Ivy asked anxiously.

"What's wrong?" I asked, before immediately realising it sounded a bit abrupt.

The librarian looked up. Her face was awash with tears. "Girls," she choked. "My library. M-my books..."

Ivy had always been better at dealing with people than me. "Miss, I don't think it spread too far... there's probably lots than can be saved. Maybe we can help you."

"They won't let me in. Apparently it's not... not safe..."

Ivy crouched down on the other side of Miss Jones. The librarian pulled out a hanky from her pocket, the word *Catastrophe* embroidered on the corner. I was pretty sure it was the only time that word had ever been embroidered on to anything.

"We've lost something too," said Ivy quietly. "Maybe it's not the end of everything, though. Life goes on. You think you can't carry on, but... you do."

I looked at my twin. She was a reflection of me, as always, but there was something older and wiser about Ivy's face than I'd ever seen in my own. It didn't take me long to realise why.

She'd lost me. She'd been through my death.

It hadn't been real, but she hadn't known that at the time. It was as real to her as the cold marble floor beneath us.

"You're right," the librarian sighed sadly. "A lot can be saved. But all those books... I can feel them burning..."

I leant back against the wall, listening to Miss Jones sobbing quietly.

It felt like there was a huge weight pressing down on me, one I didn't know if I'd ever be able to lift. The weight of every person in Rookwood, the ghosts of the past and the victims of the present. Of Miss Jones and Ivy. I might have had the power to save them, but I'd lost it.

At least things couldn't get any worse.

Chapter Thirty-One

Ivy

"I've been expelled," said Ariadne.

"What? You're... you're joking, right?"

We'd been heading back past the headmaster's office when Ariadne had walked out of the door, her eyes wide as saucers.

"No," she said. "I... I've really been expelled."

Scarlet's mouth dropped open, as did mine.

This can't be happening.

"Gosh," said Ariadne, and suddenly her legs had buckled under her and she was sitting in the middle of the corridor.

Other girls milled around her like she was an unexpected rock in a river.

I knelt down beside her, feeling numb. I didn't even know how to start processing this. "What... what happened?"

"Um," she murmured, "Mrs Knight and Mr Bartholomew, they said I was seen setting off the fire alarm, and I had a chance and I blew it, and I didn't but they don't know that, and they think I did it because, because..."

"Ariadne." I shook her gently by the shoulders. "Please. What are you trying to say?"

She took a deep, shuddering breath. "My old school," she said.

"What about your old school?" I asked.

"I was expelled."

"We know you've been expelled, but what happened at your old school?" Scarlet demanded, perhaps being less than sensitive.

"I was expelled *from my old school*," said Ariadne, and her voice was as quiet and mouse-like as the day we'd met. I struggled to hear her over the noise of the chatting girls that passed us. "There was a fire and, um, I might have been responsible."

"*Might* have?" said Scarlet.

"All right, I *was* responsible! It was stupid, really!" Her eyes filled with tears. "These girls, they bullied me every day. They stole my things and pulled my hair and kicked me, and –" she sucked in another breath – "they had this awful club that met in this old woodshed and they'd never let me in. There was this pile of dry leaves outside and I had a match and I thought, what if I lit it, just to scare them?"

I gave Scarlet a nervous sideways glance, wondering where the story was going.

"I thought I would be able to put it out," she said softly. "But the whole thing caught. There was nothing left of the shed at the end."

We stared at her, horrified.

"The girls got out," she said, apparently realising that this was an important detail. "They were fine. They came running out as soon as they saw the smoke." Then her face fell again. "But they told everyone it was me. I got kicked out. My daddy was furious."

I began to understand just what was going on. "So they think that you started the fire in the library?"

She nodded cautiously. "I didn't, I promise!" I believed her. She had no motive, no reason, and Ariadne didn't lie. "But they think I've got some sort of problem..." She stopped then, mid-sentence, mouth flapping open and closed like a fish.

I didn't know what to say, either. *Ariadne. Expelled.*

Scarlet wasn't as speechless. "What happens now?" she asked.

"I have to go and get my things," said Ariadne. "And Daddy's coming here to... to... collect me..."

She burst into tears.

I didn't think I could handle any more crying without starting myself. So instead, I reached out and took Ariadne's arm. "We'll help you," I said. "We'll find out how the fire was really started, and we'll clear your name. I promise!"

Despondently, the three of us trooped up to Ariadne's room. There was no sign of Violet – she and Rose must still be with Miss Finch, being 'questioned'. I breathed a sigh of relief that our ballet teacher had arrived in the hall when she did. If they had been taken off by Mr Bartholomew, goodness only knew what could be happening to them.

Scarlet and I helped Ariadne pack all her things into the little convoy of suitcases that had followed her into school.

None of us spoke. We couldn't bear it. I just wanted to pretend this wasn't happening.

When Ariadne's side of the dorm had been packed away, we all stood and stared at her luggage. Finally, I brought myself to look at my best friend. I must have looked stricken, because she quickly said, "It's okay. I'll be all right. I promise."

"We'll get you back," said Scarlet, and I saw that her fists were shaking.

Ariadne and I both stared at her.

"What?" she snapped, before softening slightly. "I think you're pretty great, okay? This whole thing is a joke. Mr Bartholomew started that fire, I'm sure of it. But how can we prove it?"

I nodded, breathing deep. "We'll find a way," I said.

"Thanks," Ariadne replied quietly.

But a deeper fear was stirring in my heart. What if Ariadne didn't want to come back? I wouldn't blame her. She was getting away from Rookwood, just what we'd always wanted.

She'd probably be better off without us.

That evening, we waited in the foyer for Ariadne's father to arrive. Rookwood's nervous secretary had gone home for the day, so we sat around her desk, surrounded by suitcases.

"He's going to kill me," said Ariadne, shaking her head. "I'll never hear the end of it. He's going to lock me up until I'm forty-three!"

"Fathers are like that." Scarlet shrugged. "They get over it eventually."

"Not *my* father," our friend replied darkly. "He's going to *kill* me," she said again, burying her head in her knees.

"What will we do without you?" I asked, thinking aloud.

"You helped us," said Scarlet. "We might have lost everything, but we only know what we know because of you.

So... well, thanks, that's all."

Ariadne looked up again, her expression a little brighter. "You'll solve this, won't you? For me? Prove what *he*'s done?"

We nodded. "Promise."

"And you'll write to me," she said, worriedly.

"Of course!" I gave her a weak smile, but it faded as soon as it had appeared.

There was a *thunk* as someone opened one of Rookwood's enormous front doors and stepped inside, brushing snow off their overcoat.

Ariadne stood up and I followed, bracing myself for confrontation. Ariadne was innocent, and I wouldn't let him punish her, no matter what.

The man came closer. I held my ground.

And then I realised something: he was only as tall as me.

"Ariadne! My pumpkin!" he cried.

He lifted his hat up from his face, which was round and friendly, like a bespectacled owl. He swept her up into a crushing hug.

"What *have* they done to you?" He held her out at arm's length. "I knew we should never have sent you away. Now I told your mother—" He trailed off, apparently noticing I was there. "Hallo," he said. "Who's this?"

"Um." I was a bit thrown at this point. "I'm Ivy. Nice to

meet you, Mr Flitworth, sir."

Then he caught sight of Scarlet as well. "Ooh, another one? You match!" He beamed at her.

"Scarlet," she said, nonplussed.

His attention went back to his daughter. "Darling, I don't know what this nonsense is about, I'm sure. I'll be glad to have you home. Your mother said we should have you examined for pyromaniac tendencies, but I don't believe a word of it. You're still my girl."

I realised that Ariadne hadn't said anything. Her expression was one of pure horror and embarrassment.

"Say goodbye to your little friends now, eh?"

She turned back to me. I grabbed Scarlet and dragged her up off the floor. "I'll see you soon," said Ariadne, and we all hugged each other. "Please!" she added.

"I'll have Horace carry your suitcases out," said Ariadne's father. He put a hand to his mouth and said in a stage whisper, "He's my driver, you know. Only met him last week. I don't like to go outside too much – you never know what dangers are lurking." He shot a look out of the door and shuddered a little. "Besides. Not good for the digestion."

My friend's cheeks were flushed bright red as he pulled her into another hug.

"Come on, darling," he said. "You'll be home and safe in your room again. I *knew* you weren't ready to go out in the world just yet." And then, as an afterthought, "Lovely to meet you, Sally and Irene!"

We watched, gaping, as he steered Ariadne away. She turned her head back towards us. *HELP*, she mouthed.

But then she was gone, out into the flurry of snow. The heavy door swung shut behind them.

If this day got any stranger, I wasn't sure I would cope.

We were in the darkest of spirits as we walked to dinner. Scarlet's frown hadn't left her face and I felt like a boat adrift without a rudder in an endless sea.

"I know I didn't trust her before," said Scarlet suddenly as we joined the queue, "but I was an idiot. We *needed* her. All this stuff with Mr Bartholomew and Violet and Rose – where *are* they, anyway?"

I shook my head. I had no idea. I just kept thinking that our bad luck had rubbed off on Ariadne, that she wouldn't have been expelled if it weren't for us.

"We need to find out what he's done with them," Scarlet hissed. "I wouldn't put it past him to... to..." she trailed off. *To do what Miss Fox did to her.* I knew she was thinking it.

Scarlet filled her tray with a bowl of soup and a slice of bread, and shot off towards the Richmond table. Dejected, I set off after her, and almost walked right into Nadia's big sister Meena, who had been so kind to me when I first arrived at Rookwood.

"Ivy," she said. "What's wrong?"

I suppose it was written all over my face. I balanced my tray on the end of the Evergreen table – the empty space where Violet should have been.

"My friend, Ariadne," I said, trying to keep myself from crying. "She's been expelled. They think she started the fire, but I know she didn't."

"Oh no," Meena said sadly. "I'm so sorry. That's awful."

"And that's just the start of it." I stared into the soup for a moment. "Why do we stay here, Meena? What's the point? What if I just ran away tomorrow, or begged my father to take me home?" Whether or not he'd listen was another story.

Meena looked down at her blazer, at the embroidered rook and oak tree. "I stay for my friends," she said finally. "Not just my friends, even. Everyone else. We're all in the same boat here. They need me, and I need them."

She had a point. If we somehow managed to escape, who would help Violet and Rose? Who would let the Whispers' truth be told? Who would prove Ariadne innocent?

My eyes were filling with tears. I reached into the pocket of my dress for my handkerchief, and found a folded square of paper. It was a note from Ariadne!

Ivy! All is not lost – look inside my pillow-case as soon as you can. I disobeyed Miss Jones, so kept it quiet.

Good luck! We're all counting on you.

Your friend,

Ariadne

She must have slipped it into my pocket as we hugged goodbye. And just like that, my boat had a rudder again.

Chapter Thirty-Two

SCARLET

I vy slammed her tray down on the Richmond table, sending her now-cold soup sloshing over the sides of its bowl.

"Careful, Miss Grey!" Mrs Knight frowned at her.

I gave my twin a questioning look. Her face had gone from morose to utterly cheerful in a matter of minutes. She looked manic.

"Ariadne didn't return the newspaper! She left me a note saying to check inside her pillow-case – I just did and found it there! It didn't burn in the fire, Scarlet – we still have proof that the girl died!"

I couldn't believe what I was hearing. "This is AMAZING!" I yelped. "Clever, clever Ariadne – who would have thought she'd have the guts to disobey a teacher – even one as drippy as Miss Jones!"

Ivy grinned back at me triumphantly. What had happened to my timid, goody two-shoes sister? I had always loved my twin fiercely, but this new version of her was *particularly* brilliant!

I ate my soup with glee, and I didn't even care that it tasted like cardboard.

Assembly the next day began with an unwelcome visit from the headmaster.

"We have dealt with the person... responsible for starting the fire, and they are no longer on the premises and will not be returning," he said, before moving on surprisingly quickly. "Two other girls seem to have been involved, and they are being –" a cough – "questioned. One is not a pupil at this school."

Someone in front of me put their hand up. I blinked. Who was crazy enough to question Mr Bartholomew?

"Who is she, sir?"

Penny.

Ugh. I'd almost forgotten about her. She had somehow managed to avoid suspicion after the fire, but clearly hadn't decided to tell on us so far... so was she trying to land us in it now?

The headmaster frowned. "We are trying to ascertain that." He violently brushed a speck of dust from his suit. So he didn't know who Rose was yet – and he seemed particularly annoyed about it. Miss Finch was doing an excellent job of stalling things, then – thank goodness we had her on our side.

Someone had to get Rose out of there, and I suppose it had to be us. If our hunch was right...

Lessons slowly whirred their way back to life. I'd barely slept, and had to hide my snores through boring geography and arithmetic. How could I concentrate? I was desperate to find out if the library was open again. We needed to get hold of Miss Jones and see if we could unlock her memories of the past.

At lunchtime, Ivy and I raced through our sandwiches so that we'd have enough free time to get there.

We rushed through the corridors, prompting several teachers to tell us to slow down. Everyone in the school seemed particularly on edge, paranoid that Mr Bartholomew might catch any further rules being broken.

The 'DO NOT ENTER' sign remained, but the doors were no longer locked. I peered in. "Miss Jones? Are you in there?"

After a moment, a voice echoed back, "Just a minute!"

Presently, the librarian slid into view. She was wearing a pair of long black overalls and a black shirt, together with heavy gloves. She wiped her face with the back of her arm. "Sorry," she said. "I'm starting to clean up. Apparently some of the other teachers have volunteered to help. Miss Finch will be along later." She gave a feeble smile.

Ivy nudged me. "We're sorry to bother you, Miss, but it's quite important."

"Hmm, you'd better come in, then," she said. She opened the door a little wider so that we could slip inside. "Just stick with me, and don't go near any of the... damaged... areas." *Sniff.*

As I pushed past the door, I saw what she meant. All the shelves over by the secret entrance were ruined, blackened and twisted like winter trees. The books and archives near the centre were nothing but ash – further out they were merely charred. Soot covered everything and the whole place still smelt horribly of smoke. I fought the urge to turn and run back out into the fresh air.

"The headmaster..." Miss Jones muttered. "He said we were lucky that the damage didn't spread too far. The rest of the building hasn't suffered much."

"Where do they think the fire started?" Ivy asked.

"By the newspaper archives," she said. "All that old

paper, I suppose. They told me it was a girl that started it, but –" she blinked the tears from her eyes – "I don't see why anyone would do such a thing."

"It wasn't Ariadne, Miss!" I blurted out. "She was framed. Someone else did it. Someone smashed an oil lamp deliberately and, well, we think it was Mr Bartholomew. And you might be able to help us prove it."

At the mention of his name, the librarian went deathly silent, her lips in a tight line. She looked furtively all around us, as if expecting him to jump out, and then scuttled off towards the far side of the room, where all the windows were black and grimy with smoke and soot.

I gave Ivy a puzzled look, and then we both trotted off after her. What was she doing?

I caught up and grabbed her by the sleeve. "Miss, please!"

She stopped and gave me a proper library "shh!" with a finger to her lips. She spoke quietly. "You think he was trying to destroy something?" she asked, the fear pooling in her voice.

Ivy nodded. "Miss, do you know who the Whispers are?"

"I... I don't think so..."

Ivy pulled the newspaper from her satchel. "The twenty-sixth of February, nineteen fourteen. A girl drowned here..."

That definitely got a reaction. "Oh my word," said Miss Jones, sinking down on to the ash-covered seat. At least she was wearing all black. "That *horrible* day. I tried to block it from my mind. You're saying that has something to do with this?"

"It might," I said quickly, before she could notice that technically we shouldn't be in possession of the paper. "What do you know?"

"I was very young, and I'd not been at the school that long. I didn't stay long, either. Mother moved me to another school the following year. That day was when one of the older girls, she... she was found dead, floating in the lake. Everyone was so upset."

"You need to *think*, Miss," I said. Ivy gave me a warning look, and I shot one back that I hoped said *I know what I'm doing*. "Did you see anything? Because someone thinks you did." She may not have known the Whispers, but they'd known her.

Miss Jones's eyes glazed over, as if she was trying to look back into the past. She drew little squiggles with her finger in the ash. "I don't think so. It was so long ago. How could I remember?"

"Please try," Ivy begged. And then something obviously occurred to her. "Did you talk to any of the girl's friends on that day?" I saw what she was getting at. If the Whispers thought Miss Jones knew something, she must have blabbed to one of them.

"Yes, one of them... her name was Talia, I seem to remember. I was trying to comfort her. She couldn't stop crying."

I thought through the list of names on the wall. "Talia Yahalom?"

The librarian looked at me in shock. "Y-yes, come to think of it. How did you know that?"

"Doesn't matter. What did you say to her?"

She breathed deeply. "Well, I don't... It was so long ago. I said she shouldn't cry, that it would all be all right. I said –" suddenly all the colour drained from her face – "I said the headmaster had done all he could to save her."

Now we were getting somewhere. "Why did you think that?"

"I woke early that morning, about six," she started, her eyes glazed as she remembered the past. "I wanted to get to the library to read before lessons began. Out of a window I saw Mr Bartholomew, soaking wet, running away from the lake, towards the school. I thought it was strange, but continued on my way. It must have been an hour or so later that I emerged from reading to hear the terrible news about a girl being found drowned. I presumed that when I'd seen him earlier he had been returning to the school to raise the alarm, after... after wading in to try and save her!" She put her hand to her mouth. "That's what I meant when I spoke to Talia!"

Miss Jones's voice began to rise, as the cogs turned in her brain. The realisation had well and truly dawned. "But now I remember what he said in the assembly he called to announce the death. He said the *caretaker* had found the body at six o'clock – he didn't mention being anywhere near the lake at all. But he had been! He *had*!" Her voice cracked, and the tears trickled down her face. "He didn't try to save her, did he? She died because of him!"

Chapter Thirty-Three

Ivy

I watched as Miss Jones burst into tears, and I felt sick. Sick with sadness and fear.

"You're telling me," she managed through sobs, "that he burned my library because of this? To cover up what he did by trying to destroy the newspaper archive?"

I nodded slowly. I wasn't yet certain, but everything was pointing that way. "I'm so sorry, Miss."

"Right," said Scarlet. "Stay here, get on with the clean-up, and pretend you don't remember a thing, and you should be all right."

I frowned at her. Although I was glad she was suddenly taking charge of the situation, she couldn't just order teachers around. "Scarlet..."

"*No*, Ivy, there's no time for manners! This is important. Miss Jones, you can do that, can't you?"

The librarian nodded, her face now streaked with tears.

"Good," said Scarlet. "Because I've got a plan..."

I counted the minutes until our lessons ended, and the plan could be put into action.

Unfortunately, French was the last lesson of the day and Madame Boulanger was even less impressed with Scarlet's speaking than Mrs Knight had been. She said that Scarlet was "making a mockery of the French language". I felt it was a bit rich since I wasn't sure if she was even really French. Sometimes her accent slipped and she sounded *Welsh*.

So I was left waiting outside the classroom while my twin had to stay behind, writing a page on why languages were to be taken seriously.

I stared out of the window, over the snow-covered courtyard and into the endless grounds. As I detached from the world, people began to swim through my head. *Ariadne. Violet. Rose. Our mother. The Whispers.* I would carry them along with me, for as long as it took to set them all free.

I was so lost in thought that I didn't say a word when Scarlet finally left the classroom. There was no time to waste, and she had already wasted it. But that was Scarlet – it was impossible to make her toe the line. I wasn't angry – this was too important for that. As soon as she was out, I set off in a brisk walk for the stairs.

"What are you doing?" she asked, grabbing my hand and pulling me back.

"I'm going. With you."

"No. You can't," she said. "It could go badly wrong!"

"Why?"

She stood and faced me in the hallway, arms folded. A challenge. "I tried confronting a teacher before. You know the rest, or have you forgotten? I'm not letting you get involved."

"That's because you didn't do it *right*!" I threw the newspaper back down. "You had no backup. It's safer if we're together."

"You don't know that!" She shoved me in the chest, and I stumbled backwards. "What if he locks you up? What if he kills you to keep you quiet?"

"He can't get rid of both of us," I snapped. "Father knows everything that happened before, he'd suspect immediately!"

Scarlet went silent. Then she said, quietly, "Would he?"

I stood, catching my breath.

And I saw Scarlet.

I saw right through her, her layers of fierceness peeling away to reveal everything underneath – fear, vulnerability, loneliness, abandonment. I'd been thinking about her the wrong way.

She was right; I had forgotten. I'd forgotten everything she'd been through, and began to see her just as my sister again, the constant friend and thorn in my side. I had absolutely no idea of the depths of what she'd felt, locked away in that asylum.

"I'm sorry," I whispered.

You can't erase the past. I had to learn that, and soon Mr Bartholomew would have to learn it too.

Scarlet was still coiled like a spring, and I knew I had to talk her round. This was our only chance. "I'll protect you, and you'll protect me. I promise." An inkling of an idea formed, then. "We'll tell Miss Finch. If anything goes wrong, she'll know."

Scarlet's breathing steadied, but then she started to shake her head. "I don't know if I can do this," she muttered.

I held her by the arms. "If anyone can do this, it's you. Do it for Ariadne and Violet and Rose and our mother and…"

She was still shaking her head, and I realised I was still getting it wrong.

"No, forget all of them," I said.

She looked up.

"Do it for *you*."

Chapter Thirty-Four

Scarlet

Ivy was right. Maybe I couldn't find the courage to do it for ghosts I'd never met, in memory of my mother, for a new friend, for a girl I hated.

But what if it was about me? *My* pride? *My* misery?

I had suffered like these girls had suffered, and now someone was going to *pay*.

I stopped thinking about it, kept a lid on the fear that gnawed inside me. I took a deep breath. "Right," I said. "We are going to find Miss Finch."

We found her in the studio, exhausted from having just taught a class of first years. She was perched on her piano stool, her head between her knees. But however tired she was, her ears pricked up when we told her that we needed to talk to her.

Miss Finch was scared, I could tell. She said that she'd managed to smooth over the issue of finding out who Rose was by telling the other teachers that she would handle it, but it couldn't be prolonged much further. And she said we needed to keep away from Mr Bartholomew, to stay away, stay quiet, stay out of trouble.

When I was sure no one was listening, I told her everything we'd found out, and what Miss Jones had witnessed. And we told her about the task we'd given Miss Jones. Miss Finch wasn't happy that we were going to put ourselves in such danger, but she was aghast at what we'd discovered and pledged to help in any way she could.

And so, with our insurance in place, we were ready. I sincerely hoped Mr Bartholomew was *not* ready for us.

Knock knock.

I clenched my stomach, fighting the urge to be sick. With that knock, there was no going back. The word 'HEADMASTER' loomed down at me from the door.

There was no answer. I looked at Ivy. Her face was a mask,

and I could tell she was pretending not to be terrified.

Play your cards close to your chest. I repeated these words over and over to myself.

Knock knock.

I felt as though my heart were about to drop through my chest. *He could still give us a caning*, my mind warned, before I told it to shut up. *He could—*

The door opened.

Mr Bartholomew stood there, his face etched with a frown. "Students are not permitted to knock at my door... unless explicitly told to by a teacher." He sounded like he was reading from the rulebook. I expected he was just about to reel off a punishment, but Ivy interrupted him.

"Sir, we need to talk to you. I think you'd prefer it if it was private."

"How *dare* you presume to speak to me in this manner?" The expression on his wrinkled face was white-hot with fury.

Ivy frowned back, and I saw her defiance edge ahead of her fear. "Twenty-sixth of February, nineteen fourteen," she said quietly.

The headmaster's face went the colour of sour milk, like the drowned girl herself had appeared in front of him. He stepped back into the room, giving us an opening. We pushed our way into the office, vast, dark and stinking of pipe smoke. The door swung shut behind us.

"You shouldn't be in here..." he started, but it set off his coughing, and he folded into a hunch.

"We've come to bargain," I retorted, sounding braver than I felt.

"Bargain with what?" he growled. He shouldered past us to the blazing fireplace, fumbling for the poker.

"What we know," I said. "You heard the date Ivy said. We know exactly what you did, sir. You thought you could just get away with it?"

He swung back to us, his grizzled frown turning into a snarl. "What do you think you know?" He had the poker in his hand, the tip red-hot, and he held it pointed towards me.

I was just going to tell it straight, but something flipped inside me. There was anger longing to escape, and suddenly I knew how we were going to get a reaction.

I made my face as blank as possible, and fixed my eyes to a space in thin air just to the left of Mr Bartholomew.

"You did it, sir. You sent me out there, to the lake. Told me it was for my own good. It was so cold and so dark, sir. I was frightened. I didn't want to do it." I spoke in a whisper, unearthly and strange.

"No," he said, backing away, shaking his head. "No, you can't..."

"You said it was a punishment, but it was more than that, wasn't it? You wanted the control. You wouldn't let me stop.

But I couldn't carry on, and the current pulled me under... you held *me under, sir—"*

"NO!" he roared and he thrust the poker towards me.

But Ivy darted in front of me, and grabbed it. I heard a sickening fizzle as the heat bit into her skin, but it was only for a moment – she wrenched it off him and threw it to the floor.

Mr Bartholomew dropped to his knees, and a coughing fit racked his body, the most dreadful I had heard. It sounded like it was scraping his lungs, pulling out his insides. He clutched at his chest.

We stood, and we watched him. Watched him choke and fight for his breath on the carpet.

"This is what you did to her," said Ivy.

But it didn't get that far. The fit passed, and he spat on the carpet, then wiped his mouth on his jacket sleeve. He dragged himself back, leaning against his desk, gasping for air. "What. Do. You. Want?"

"We want justice. We want you locked away for the crimes you've committed in this school over the years. We want to finish the work that the Whispers in the Walls began!"

"And we want Ariadne Flitworth reinstated," Ivy demanded. "We know *you* started that fire to destroy the newspaper section! We heard you creeping around the library when Miss Jones helped us find the edition from the day the girl drowned. You must have realised that we were getting too close to the truth. We're going to take the evidence of what you've done straight to the police!"

His eyes were streaming, his face haggard. "There is no evidence," he growled. "That girl, she was *disrespectful* and badly behaved, just as you are. She needed to be taught a lesson. *All of them* needed to. I taught them a lesson they would *never* forget." His fury radiated off him in waves.

"So you admit it?" I said, raising my voice. "You killed her?"

"I KILLED HER," he roared, finally catching his breath. "AND I'LL KILL YOU TOO IF I GET THE CHANCE!"

Without a word, I walked over to the door and opened it.

And when the policeman stepped in, the look on Mr Bartholomew's face was *priceless*.

Chapter Thirty-Five

IVY

We'd had Miss Jones call the village police and, after she'd explained everything, they'd come as quickly as they could. And, just as we'd hoped, they'd been able to listen as the headmaster confessed.

We stood back and watched as they led Mr Bartholomew away in handcuffs. His eyes were sunken, and he finally looked defeated. Scarlet gave him her fiercest, most defiant glare.

Miss Jones and Miss Finch were standing together in

the corridor, both of them with worried expressions on their faces.

"We need to tell Violet and Rose that they're safe!" I said.

Miss Finch nodded. "Come with me, I'll take you to them."

We made our way to the stairs. We pushed our way through a group of girls that were gathered there halfway up. Josephine and Ethel looked at us suspiciously. Violet had been their friend once. I wondered if they cared about her at all now.

Miss Finch had trouble climbing the stairs – she clung to the banister, and by the time we reached the first floor she was out of breath. "Go on ahead," she said. "Find them. Come and get me if you need me."

I looked at my twin. "Scarlet, my hand..."

We weren't far from the bathrooms. "Run it under the cold water," said Miss Finch, leaning back against the wall.

So as quick as I could, I shot into the bathrooms and turned a tap on. The water came out spluttering at first, but soon it was running clear. I held my hand under it. *Bliss*. The burn wasn't too bad, and it wasn't long before it was soothed.

Another girl was in there, and she gave me a sideways look, as if wondering what I was doing. "Spilt tea on it," I said quickly. Where I would have got tea that was any hotter than lukewarm from at Rookwood, I had no idea, but she seemed placated by the explanation and turned away.

I ran back out again. Scarlet was waiting by the stairs. "Come on," she said. And then, after a pause, she screwed up her face. "Sometimes even the witch needs rescuing."

On the almost-empty top floor, we shouted Violet's name, heard it echo off the walls. And as we reached one end, a response.

"We're in here!"

The door was bolted from the outside. I slid it back and we threw the door open.

The room held some old chairs and tables – and the chairs held Violet and Rose.

"Did Miss Finch send you?" Violet sniffed. "How did you find us?"

"Mr Bartholomew has been arrested," I said. "You're free to go."

"Really?" said Violet, standing up. She looked exhausted, dark shadows under her eyelids, the same soot-stained clothes she'd been wearing the night of the fire. An air of mistrust crept into her voice. "Are you sure? This isn't some trick?"

"Not a trick," I promised, before Scarlet could open her mouth and convince them otherwise. "Rose is safe, for now."

Rose looked up from the chair, where she'd been rocking

back and forth. Her expression said *me*?

I nodded to her. She looked at Violet – wanting to know that everything was okay, I supposed. Violet smiled back at her, and I think it was the first time I'd ever seen her look happy.

But then her expression turned to puzzlement. "So who started the fire?" she said.

"It was the headmaster," I told her. "Though he didn't actually confess to that part."

She looked at me like I was mad. "Why would he set fire to his own school?"

"It's a long story," I said, and it really was.

"What do I do now?" Violet asked us. She looked like a lost little girl. Rose reached out and gently touched her hand.

"Well, you've got a room to yourself now," said Scarlet. Violet seemed unfazed by this news. "Rose could stay there. Now that Mr Bartholomew is out of the picture, the teachers aren't as likely to go along with his cover-ups."

"We'll work things out," I assured them.

Slowly, Rose got to her feet, still clad in Penny's clothes, now very tattered and smoke-damaged. She stepped towards us, and looked us in the eye.

"Thank you," she said.

Violet and Rose returned to Violet's room, Rose stepping

into it daintily and cautiously as if she wasn't quite sure if the floor was solid.

Miss Finch stood in the doorway with us, watching them.

"Please, Miss," said Violet. "Can she really stay here? I don't want her family to lock her away again."

"I suppose," said Miss Finch. Rose smiled pleasantly. "Until we find somewhere more suitable. At least it's not the basement. I don't know if she'll be allowed in lessons, though. Perhaps she could help out in the stables."

That raised a bigger grin from Rose. Suddenly, she pulled out a book from her cardigan pocket.

It had a pony on the cover.

Chapter Thirty-Six

SCARLET

I savoured my dinner that night. It was roast pork – or, well, Rookwood's attempt at roast pork, anyway. But at least I was alive to taste it.

Rose was allowed to come to the dining hall, although most of the teachers couldn't quite fathom why she was there. They made a place for her on the Evergreen table with Violet, and she wolfed down her food in the way you'd expect from someone who'd been half-starved for weeks.

I turned back and saw Mrs Knight talking to Miss Danver,

the physics teacher. They talked quickly and quietly, their faces white. Mrs Knight must have been spreading the word about Mr Bartholomew. I wondered when the announcement about him would be made. For now, I kept our triumphant secret to myself.

Ivy sat beside me, and she seemed to be (almost) enjoying her food too. Both of us tried our hardest to ignore the empty seat.

But Penny, as always, had to make life difficult. "I see your little friend got kicked out," she sneered as she set her tray down. "It should have been the lot of you. And Violet too."

I raised my fork at her, about to start yelling. I'd had enough that day without Penny being her usual hideous self. But Ivy stepped in.

"Look, Penny," she said, her voice weary. "Have you tried just... talking to Violet? Asking her what she went through?"

Penny went still, her expression blank. I think she was deciding whether or not to answer.

But Ivy continued. "All this has been because you think Violet betrayed you, stopped being your friend. Did you ever think that maybe you weren't being a good friend to her?"

"I didn't—" Penny argued, but Ivy was having none of it.

"Pull yourself together," she snapped. "She nearly *died* because of your petty squabbling. You nearly got us all in deep, deep trouble with the headmaster. And all because of your jealousy!"

Penny went silent.

I stared at my twin, open-mouthed. Some days it was like I didn't even recognise her. Where had she found the courage to speak to Penny like that? She'd always let me do the talking when we were younger.

Everyone had stopped talking, paying attention to Ivy, knowing something dramatic was happening. I thought they'd all go back to chatting in a minute, while Penny stewed in her own juices.

And then suddenly, Nadia leant forward. "Ivy's right," she said defiantly. "You need to get over it. We're all sick of you two fighting, and you being a complete grump about everything!"

Murmurs of agreement spread down the table.

Penny flushed bright red. She stood up, her chair scraping back on the floor. Was she about to scream at us?

But no, to the surprise of just about everyone, she was walking across the hall, through the rabble, to where Violet sat.

We couldn't hear what she said, but we all stared nonetheless. And we all saw when Violet reached out her arm and shook Penny's hand.

Finally, there was a truce.

*

I slept soundly that night, considering. I feared the return of the nightmare, but it didn't come. As I woke, I wondered sleepily if it had been a message.

I shook my head. I know I've been cooped up in here too long when I start believing in that nonsense.

At the end of assembly, they handed out letters – and I was surprised to hear our names called.

I went to the front to pick it up, and afterwards in the corridor I eagerly tore it open. What it could it be? Ivy hovered beside me, curious.

As soon as I pulled it out of the brown envelope, though, I recognised the handwriting. Aunt Phoebe.

Dear Scarlet and Ivy,

I am missing you both dearly. I think, perhaps, I was a bit rash in agreeing with your stepmother. I hope you do not feel abandoned. I was thinking of asking her and your father if you would be allowed to stay with me during the Christmas holidays. I don't know if they will agree, but just so you know, I will try.

Ivy, dear – where did I leave the shovel? I just can't think where it could be…

Your aunt
Phoebe Gregory

I grinned at my twin, and I was pleased to see her mirroring the grin back at me. We headed off to our first lesson – double Latin, ugh – but there was a spring in our step, and Ivy had already pulled out her ink pen to write a reply.

"Aunt Phoebe," she muttered. "The shovel is in the shed, where it always has been..."

In lessons I really began to feel the loss of Ariadne. It was a lot quieter without her around. And as I watched Ivy, carefully writing out her Latin grammar, I saw a tear roll down her cheek. She missed our friend too.

At break time I spotted Mrs Knight trotting through the corridor.

"Miss," I said, almost running to keep up with her, "can Ariadne come back to school now that Mr Bartholomew's been arrested?"

She stopped, and a weak smile crossed her face. "I'm afraid not, my dear. I telephoned her parents, but they don't want her to return."

"Why not?"

Her eyes crinkled at the corners, and I could tell she was deciding whether or not to tell me. "They're unhappy about her being accused of starting the fire. And they think the school is... unsuitable." With that, she gave a curt nod and started to walk away.

"Miss..." I said, and she stopped mid-step.

"What is it, Scarlet? I have a lot to do at the moment!"

"Ariadne should be here. She deserves to be here, much more than I do. She's actually a good student. And a good person. She's pretty good at everything, really."

Mrs Knight sighed, and I swore I saw a hint of genuine sadness in her eyes. "Perhaps so. But you'll have to take that up with her parents, I'm afraid."

She left me standing in the corridor, and I wondered how I was going to tell Ivy.

"Let's go," I said, as the bell rang out for the end of the day, taking my twin's arm.

"Go where?" she asked, a frown still etched on her face. I'd told her what Ariadne's parents had said, and she wasn't happy.

"Go and do something Ariadne would do. *Investigate*."

It was something that had been playing on my mind, ever since I'd read those words in the newspaper.

Ivy protested continually as I took her up to our room and we pulled on our warmest clothes. "Why?" she kept saying. "What are we looking for?" But I didn't want to say, not just yet.

All right, I was playing with her, I'll admit it...

Outside, the snow was a few days old. Some of it was melting, some brown around the edges. Footprints criss-crossed it, mud and gravel peeked through from the ground below.

I set off towards the lake.

"Scarlet, this is ridiculous!" Ivy shouted after me. "Tell me what you're looking for!"

"Got a hunch!" I shouted back.

Together we trudged over the frosty ground, our breath forming little steam clouds. Ivy kept huffing, and it made me laugh. I stopped in my tracks, bent down and scooped up a handful of snow, and hurled it right at her.

"Ack!" she yelled in frustration.

I laughed again, and carried on walking. Seconds later, a snowball hit me in the back of the head. I looked round to see my twin grinning wickedly.

Finally, we pushed through the copse and came to the lake. "Now we start looking," I said. "But I really don't know where to start."

"*You* don't know where to start? I don't even know what we're looking *for*!" Ivy pouted at me.

"You'll know when you see it."

So we wandered around the shore, picking through the undergrowth. It had to be near here – didn't it?

As I stepped up on to a rock, I caught sight of my

reflection in the icy lake. I looked mad, certainly. Maybe I was, out here looking for something when I had no idea if it was even there.

But in the horrible cold, I could see the truth. I'd never been mad, never been insane. I knew exactly what I was doing. I knew what was real in the world.

As I had that realisation and stepped down into frosty brambles, I stubbed my toe on something. I kicked some of the branches away, knelt down and inspected it closely.

IN LOVING MEMORY

"Ivy!" I called. "Found it!"

The article in the newspaper had said that a plaque would be erected for the girl who drowned. And here it was, right in front of me. It was brass, worn and scratched, covered in twigs and leaves.

Ivy tramped through the undergrowth to where I was kneeling down. "Oh," she said quietly. "That's what you were looking for."

But I wasn't done. There had to be a name, didn't there? If we knew her name, we could put her to rest.

I reached out with gloved hands and began to pull off the debris, until the bottom of the plaque was clear.

And then I froze. And I stopped breathing.

OF EMMELINE ADEL

Chapter Thirty-Seven

Ivy

 y mouth dropped open. "No," was all I could say. "No. That can't be right."

Scarlet stood up and backed away from the plaque, her hand covering her lips. "I don't... I don't understand," she said.

Our mother.

Our mother who had been a member of the Whispers.

Our mother who had died not long after we were born.

Our mother who had died in a lake, drowned at the hands of the headmaster...

It wasn't possible. No one could die twice.

What was real? Suddenly I had no idea. I fumbled for an explanation, for something to say. "It must have been a different person, with the same name."

Scarlet just pointed at the bottom of the plaque.

05.01.1899 — 26.02.1914
GONE BUT NOT FORGOTTEN

That was her birthday.

I sat down on the chilly rock, without even realising what my legs were doing. I propped up my head with my hands, just staring at my twin.

"It's a prank," she said finally. "Someone's messing with us." But even she didn't sound convinced. She knew as well as I did that no one at the school knew our mother's name, especially not her maiden name. And besides, the thing looked easily weathered enough to have been there for over twenty years.

I shook my head, and stared out over the icy surface of the lake.

After some thought, I spoke again. "I think there are only two possible explanations. Either she faked her own death, or whoever our mother really was, she wasn't Emmeline Adel. She was someone else. An imposter."

There was a look of shock on my twin's face that I was sure mirrored my own. But it gradually melted, and suddenly she was laughing.

"What?" I asked indignantly.

"Well, you can see where we get it from, can't you?"

I fought so hard not to laugh back. "Scarlet, this is serious..."

She only grinned harder and waved her arms, sending nearby rooks shrieking from the trees. "Don't you see? She was just like us. Maybe we don't know what happened, but... maybe she pretended to die to escape Mr Bartholomew. Or maybe she swapped identities with the real Emmeline. Whoever she was, she was *smart*, and her life was just as crazy as ours!"

I sighed, trying to imagine the woman I'd only ever seen in a stiff old photograph as a young girl. Now I wanted to know her more than ever. The *real* her. What had she been through? Why had she done these things?

And another, more pressing question came to mind. "Do you think Father had any idea?"

"That clueless old boot? I doubt it. He didn't even tell us that she went here, did he? You'd think that would occur to him, since he shipped us off to this school."

"I hope you're right," I said. "I mean, if Father knew anything about the headmaster, he *really* shouldn't have

291

sent us here."

We both fell silent for a moment, considering that perhaps he had known and just *didn't care*. But that thought was too awful, too painful, and I brushed it aside.

"Maybe we'll get the chance to ask him someday," I continued.

"You can ask," said Scarlet. "Next time I see him, I'm going to tell him *exactly* what I think of him."

I smiled. That was an event I didn't want to miss.

As I lay in bed that night, watching the frost climb the window, I vowed two things to myself:

1.   I would get Ariadne back.
2.   I would find out who our mother really was.

It couldn't be *that* hard. Could it?

Those thoughts were the ones floating around my head that Saturday morning. Scarlet had returned to our room after breakfast, but I wanted to go back to the library and make sure Miss Jones was all right.

And on the way there, I stopped. Right outside Miss Fox's office door.

It was open again, but there were no suited men inside this time.

I don't know what made me do it, but I took a step over

the threshold. Although the men had taken all her papers and files, the room seemed otherwise untouched. I stood in the middle of the floor, and I looked around. The dogs in their frames stared down at me. Still, silent. The stuffed dogs remained too, and their downcast faces surrounded me. All of them.

All but one.

Once, when I'd been trapped in the office when Miss Fox decided a punishment for Penny and I, I'd counted all of the stuffed dogs. There had been eight.

Now there were seven.

I frowned, counting again, thinking I must have missed one. But no, there were only seven of the poor things. And then it struck me – *the Chihuahua*. The one that had sat on her desk, with pens in its mouth. It was gone. I peered closer. There were little dusty outlines where its paws had been.

I leant back. Someone must have taken it out. Maybe they cleared it away when they were going through her desk. That had to be it. It didn't mean anything.

I stepped out of the office. I shut the door.

And I ran away as fast as my legs would carry me.

Chapter Thirty-Eight

Scarlet

I stared into the mirror, and the mirror stared back.

It had always been Ivy that I saw there before, but now I wondered how much of our mother I was seeing. My hair, my eyes – what was hers?

There was one thing I felt sure was hers. Spirit. Rebellion. I held up my chin with pride. Whoever she had been, whoever the real Emmeline Adel had been, she fought for what she believed in.

And that's when I had the idea.

It took some time to talk myself round. It was something

that terrified me, deeply. *But come on*, I told myself, *you're Scarlet Grey. You're not scared.*

It was one thing to say it in my head, and another to act on it. I was shaking as I tore a page out of the back of my diary and wrote a note –

Gone to the roof. Be back soon.

I pulled on my gloves and coat.

I took the stairs one at a time, slowly, savouring my safety. I felt my heart quicken, though I tried to calm it. No matter how much I told myself it was fine, my body didn't believe me. When I reached the top, my lungs were gasping for air.

I stopped at the hatch, sat down on the floor beneath it. *I can do this. Nothing bad will happen. It's just a roof.*

I don't know how long I was sitting there, staring up at the hatch, at the glimpse of swirling white sky. I was almost in a trance of panic, not wanting to move. The roof was the source of all my fears. Where it had all gone so, so wrong.

However long it was, the trance was shattered by the sound of footsteps pounding up the stairs. I struggled to my feet.

"Scarlet?" Ivy panted.

There was something in her expression... she looked horrified.

"What's wrong?" I asked.

She stopped, leant against the banister. She gazed up at me for a moment too long. "Nothing," she said finally. "It's nothing. What are you doing up here?"

I pointed at the roof hatch, as if that explained everything.

"But it's snowing..." Ivy started. She didn't finish the sentence, though. I supposed she'd seen the determination on my face.

"I need to go up there," I said. "I can't be afraid any more. I just can't!"

I was expecting her either to tell me it was easy or to tell me I was being ridiculous. What I didn't expect was what she actually said:

"Let's do it. Together."

I gave her a questioning look, but she nodded. She meant it.

Ivy went over to the roof hatch and pulled on the still-unlocked padlock. The hatch swung open, and she climbed out. Then she leant back down and held out her hand.

I drank in a deep breath. Maybe I could be scared on my own, but I couldn't be scared in front of Ivy.

I took her hand.

And I stepped out on to the roof.

The vertigo hit me first. I reeled, trying not to look. The ground was such a *long* way down.

"Scarlet, it's all right," said Ivy. And then, "Scarlet, look!"

The urgency in her voice caught my attention, even though I was trying to hide my face. I looked up and saw what she was pointing at.

Perched on a chimney pot, in the falling snow, was a barn owl. It stared back at me, something old and wise about its face.

I opened my mouth, speechless. Before we could move, the owl had leapt into the air, its wings spread wide. It flew away from the roof, over...

The world.

The snow covered everything. It was like someone had drained the world of all colour except black, white, and the icy blue of the sky reflected in the frozen lake.

The owl swooped towards the ground, a dark shadow over the white world.

Once I'd looked, I couldn't look away.

"Nothing's going to happen," said Ivy, but I wasn't listening.

I made it.

I got back on to the rooftop, after everything. The place that had been mine, before it was taken from me. Before I saw it only in my nightmares.

Well, I was going to claim it back. Right now.

The snow was deep and compacted. Our footprints had

barely made a dent in it. That was good. I could do what I set out to do. I began scooping out the snow in lines. At first, my twin just stared at me, but after a while she started to help, following my lead. I think she realised what I was up to.

When we'd finally finished, I stood back, careful not to knock any of it out of place.

I looked down at what we'd written.

THE WHISPERS HAVE BEEN HEARD

Acknowledgements

I'm so thrilled to have had the chance to bring Scarlet and Ivy back together. But I have of course had a lot of help along the way with wrangling Rookwood School into shape for a second time, and these are the people I need to thank:

My amazing editor duo – Lauren Fortune who worked so hard on the majority of the book with me, and Lizzie Clifford who was a huge help in the planning of the story. The whole team at HarperCollins who have helped to build the books and get them to readers (and know how to throw the best parties). Manuel Šumberac for his brilliant illustrations, capturing the world of Rookwood perfectly. Super-agent Jenny Savill and all the team of lovely folk at Andrew Nurnberg Associates. My "writer support group" a.k.a. the Bath Spa MA Writing For Young People gang, r/YA Writers and the #ukmgchat-ers on Twitter – what would I do without you lot?

Special thanks must go to my family, friends and my husband, for all the love and support. I owe you all a pizza.

A final, world-turtle-sized thank you to Sir Terry Pratchett, whose books shaped my life and writing in many ways.

And, as always, thank you for reading.